Royals in the H...

It's their duty...to wed!

Breaking news: newly crowned King Sebastian and
reformed rebel Prince Alessio are headed to the altar.
They're short just one thing—a bride!

Determined to redeem his scandalous past and
prove he's worthy of his title, Alessio promises to
rejuvenate Celiana's tourism with a bride lottery.
And the lucky winner will become his princess!

Brie never expected to win. Her name was only in
the running as a publicity stunt to promote her
fledgling marketing business. Now she's engaged
to a prince and #lottobride is trending!

From birth, Sebastian was destined to take the
throne. But being perfect never earned him the love
he craved. Now he'll commit himself to a life of duty
only, which means a marriage of convenience
with local aristocrat Lady Breanna...

Breanna has always put everyone else's happiness
ahead of her own. Yet her unexpected chemistry
with Sebastian makes her wish their fairy-tale royal
wedding could be for more than just the cameras...

Find out what happens behind palace doors in
Juliette Hyland's debut for Harlequin Romance!

Prince Alessio and Brie's story
How to Win a Prince

King Sebastian and Lady Breanna's story
How to Tame a King

Both available now!

Dear Reader,

When I wrote the princess lottery in *How to Win a Prince*, I knew I had to come back and give King Sebastian his happy ending. And to find his queen, I looked no farther than the princess lottery! Like Princess Brie, the lottery was the last place Breanna Galanis wanted to be.

Breanna spent her whole life as the two-for-one special—an identical twin to grasping parents yearning for aristocratic titles. When the sisters' names aren't drawn in the princess lottery, Breanna starts planning their escape. The only problem... King Sebastian shows up demanding a bride. So Breanna protects her sister and weds a king.

King Sebastian was born to rule. It's the only thing he knows. He's accepted the crown and its burdens. But he needs a partner. One who's happy with a marriage of convenience in exchange for a crown. And who better than one of the Galanis twins, who desperately wanted to wed his brother? A queen's crown is better than a princess's, right? But what happens when the last thing his queen actually wanted was the crown he put on her head?

Enjoy King Sebastian and his queen's royal happily-ever-after!

Juliette Hyland

HOW TO TAME A KING

JULIETTE HYLAND

ROMANCE

Harlequin®
ROMANCE

Recycling programs for this product may not exist in your area.

ISBN-13: 978-1-335-59673-4

How to Tame a King

Copyright © 2024 by Juliette Hyland

Harlequin Enterprises ULC
22 Adelaide St. West, 41st Floor
Toronto, Ontario M5H 4E3, Canada
www.Harlequin.com

Printed in U.S.A.

Juliette Hyland believes in strong coffee, hot drinks and happily-ever-afters! She lives in Ohio with her Prince Charming, who has patiently listened to many rants regarding characters failing to follow the outline. When not working on fun and flirty happily-ever-afters, Juliette can be found spending time with her beautiful daughters and giant dogs, or sewing uneven stitches with her sewing machine.

Books by Juliette Hyland

Harlequin Romance

Royals in the Headlines
How to Win a Prince

Harlequin Medical Romance

Hope Hospital Surgeons
Dating His Irresistible Rival
Her Secret Baby Confession

Boston Christmas Miracles
A Puppy on the 34th Ward

The Prince's One-Night Baby
Rules of Their Fake Florida Fling
Redeeming Her Hot-Shot Vet
Tempted by Her Royal Best Friend

Visit the Author Profile page at Harlequin.com.

For Doreen.
Congrats on your retirement; enjoy this next stage!

Praise for
Juliette Hyland

"A delightful second chance on love with intriguing characters, powerful back stories and tantalizing chemistry! Juliette Hyland quickly catches her reader's attention.... I really enjoyed their story! I highly recommend this book.... The story line has a medical setting with a whole lot of feels in the mix!"

—*Goodreads* on
Falling Again for the Single Dad

CHAPTER ONE

BREANNA GALANIS WAS glad she hadn't shared her doubts about her identical twin sister Anastasia's room design as she looked at the striped accent wall blurring into bright colors. It was striking. Not at all the gaudy image her mind had conjured when Annie had described it. Her sister's talent was wasted in the high walls of the Galanis family compound.

"This is gorgeous." Breanna clapped.

"I told you." Annie snapped a few pictures with her phone, then pulled the professional camera hanging around her neck to her eye. Her finger clicked over and over.

"You did." She wasn't sure their parents would approve, but then, she didn't know the last time they'd approved of anything the twins did. That didn't stop their mother from showing off the new designs to her friends.

They all assumed she'd found a hot new designer—and each had begged for their name. Her mother had refused to say it was Anastasia.

Whether it was to make her friends jealous that she had access to something they craved or because she didn't want them to find out about Annie's gift, Breanna didn't know.

Probably both. Image mattered, after all. More than anything else in her parents' orbit.

Galanis women married well. They didn't have careers. Their job was to host parties, be armpieces and proof of the lavish wealth others coveted. In other words, showpieces in designer clothes, worn once and tossed away.

Aristocrats without titles—according to her father.

The view was outdated. After all, they were well into the twenty-first century. Breanna had wanted to run from their parents' control for years. She had her degree in early childhood education. She loved children, and would have been in the profession for years now if her parents hadn't intervened at every place she'd interviewed. She was also a skilled seamstress who thrifted and upcycled clothes, despite her parents' disgust of the "trade." She could sell clothes, teach classes, and Annie could open a design studio. Their life would be simple compared to the extravagant wealth they'd grown up with, but their lives would finally be theirs.

Anastasia wanted more of a plan. More concrete proof they'd be all right. She wanted a full portfolio of room decor designs before they left.

So far, she'd remodeled ten rooms in the mansion, plus her and Breanna's bedrooms. This was the fourth "final" room.

"It's perfect." Breanna bit her lip, then forced her shoulders back. "And it's the last one, right?"

They could make a go of it. They just had to take the first step.

Annie's hands shook, and she lowered the camera. The happiness drained from her body as she looked at the colorful walls around her. Her gaze focused everywhere but on Breanna. "I was looking at my portfolio this morning. I don't have a kitchen yet."

"Annie…"

"I know. I know I said this was the last one. But we will have nothing. Mother and Father will cut us off completely. You tried to get a teaching position years ago. Father blocked it. He *will* do it again." Her voice caught, and she pinched her eyes closed. "People will balk at hiring me too, but design work… I can run my own business. Give us some income."

"I have my sewing. They can't take that. They can't control everything." Breanna said it with more certainty than she felt. What was the price of freedom?

"And we won't be alone. We'll have each other." Breanna was the younger sister by all of two minutes, but she'd always protected Anastasia. Annie was the one with the big dreams.

The one who had plans…if she'd only start down the path.

Breanna was the extra. The interchangeable twin who asked too many questions but never pushed too far. Hell, she'd even accepted it when her parents gave large donations to the institutions she'd applied to not to hire her.

Breanna was determined that Annie got to have dreams outside the compound. She was too talented to stay. Too talented to only be someone's wife. Love, if it really existed, was wonderful—at least according to the storybooks.

Her parents treated their union like a chess game. A winner and loser, constantly making moves and trying to stay at least three steps ahead of each other. A winner and a loser and two daughters who looked identical for them to trade for the best offer.

Unless they left. "Annie—a kitchen?"

"Is a necessity in any portfolio. I have everything else. I should have seen it."

Breanna tilted her head and raised a brow. Annie had studied portfolios for months when coming up with the brilliant plan to ready her portfolio under her parents' careful watch.

Getting them to agree to redo their kitchen would be a lot of work. And a kitchen renovation…it would add months to the plan. Maybe even a year. They'd gotten lucky at Prince Alessio's Princess Lottery last year.

Prince Alessio had spent a year raising money for the arts by funding a princess lottery—with the prize to be his wife. Each week the price of the ticket had increased. The total cost for a year's entry was well over ten thousand pounds. Annie and Breanna were the only participants with a year's worth of entries. Statistically, one of their names should have popped out. Yet the universe had chosen another and given Prince Alessio and his new wife, Princess Brie, a happily-ever-after.

That kind of luck wouldn't last. Their parents would try again to find them a title. They needed to leave.

"Annie—we can—"

The door opened, and the twins snapped to attention as their father walked in. He was smiling. No. Their father routinely walked into rooms already halfway through an argument, but right now he was beaming. Glowing even. Whatever he was about to say would be bad news—for them.

It made her skin crawl. Lucas Galanis did not beam. His smiles were calculated to win a business deal. Whatever calculation he'd made, he planned to win today. Which meant she and Annie lost.

"Guess what, Anastasia?" The peppy words sounded congratulatory, but the authoritarian tone he used wasn't hidden. Her sister hated the use of her full name, but only Breanna ever called her Annie.

It wouldn't be hard for their parents to adopt the nickname, but in the Galanis family, everything was tinged with power. Annie preferred her nickname; therefore, the most powerful members of the family would refuse to use it.

Annie rocked a little and lowered her head. "What?"

"You're going to be the queen." His words were wrong. They had to be.

King Sebastian wasn't even looking for a bride. Though the press seemed to think every woman in his orbit was his future queen. One woman had even taken a job overseas just to stop the press from hounding her after an image of Sebastian smiling at her during a dinner function went viral.

The man was simply living his life. Except, *nothing to see here* did not sell ad space. Since Prince Alessio and Brie's happy union, the crown had been dull.

Sebastian had had a brief rebellious streak following his father's death. But most of those headlines were drowned out by Alessio's bride lottery. And the rebel Sebastian, whoever he'd been, had disappeared months ago. In his stead was the prince, turned king, she'd followed all her life.

The man was stoic. If the dictionary needed a picture of *duty* beside it, they could use King

Sebastian. He never missed a meeting. Never stepped out of place at an event.

And never smiled.

"I can't be queen." Annie's words were barely a whisper, but their father heard them.

His smile slipped into the sneer Breanna knew so well. "King Sebastian chose you."

"He doesn't know her." Breanna's fingernails dug into her palms. There had to be a way out of this.

But if the king wanted one of them… The heat of the warm evening evaporated. Cold seeped through her body as she tried to piece together any plan. Breanna worked the system that was their family better than Annie. But in the chess game of her family, her father was the grand master.

Which was why all she had were *plans* to leave. Fancy ideas. A small bank account for a few months' rent. Thoughts. Discussion points. All of which were good. Until your bluff was called.

They needed to stand firm. The moment was here, and they had to rise to the occasion.

Now. Or never.

"He doesn't need to know her." What a sad, flippant statement. How could their father treat marriage, a lifelong commitment, supposedly, with so little concern? This was Annie's life.

But their parents didn't care about their daughters' lives. According to them, they'd been blessed with two identical beauties to give them access to a world that hadn't wanted them. Being rich beyond anyone's wildest dreams should have been enough. But Lucas and Matilda Galanis wanted titles. If they couldn't have them, then their daughters would.

Breanna looked to Annie, but her sister wouldn't meet her gaze. Her palm ached, but Breanna pressed on. She couldn't lose this round to her father. "He is marrying her. He needs to know her. To love…"

Red patches bloomed on her father's cheeks. She'd gone too far, but stopping wasn't an option. Not this time.

"Love is a childish game that gets you nowhere."

"Prince Alessio loves Princess Brie." Annie's head didn't lift as she pushed a tear away. At least she'd said something.

Their father's scoff carried in the beautiful room. "That isn't real. It's a media game. And even if it is real, what has he gotten from it? Outcast to a glass shop?"

Breanna personally thought Alessio and his "lotto bride," as everyone had initially called her, looked happier than ever. All the pictures were of them laughing or looking at each other like no one else's opinions mattered. Like the headlines that ran about them in the early days calling Brie all sorts of names were beneath their love.

Maybe that was staged, but it looked like Alessio had gotten freedom.

And it wasn't like they were thrown out of the royal family. Far from it, in fact. Alessio still regularly attended events. Brie was a constant presence on the tourism boards. He just had a life outside of the palace. A life of his own.

Something King Sebastian and his queen would never have.

Annie drew a deep breath, and Breanna knew what the resignation on her soft features meant. No. No. No.

The discussion of the room's design seemed so long ago now. In a place far away. The dream was floating away. It would be out of reach if Annie acquiesced.

"I'll do it." Breanna's voice was stronger than she expected. Stronger than she felt.

"Breanna."

She didn't look at Annie. If she did, she might let the tears pushing against her eyes fall. That could not happen. Breanna protected Annie. That was her role. She would not fail now that it truly mattered.

"If he doesn't need to know Anastasia, then he doesn't need to know me." Annie still had a chance for her dreams. She could make this happen, and if Breanna was queen, she could protect her twin.

As queen, she could ensure Annie's safety.

Their father tilted his head, weighing his options. A weird feeling as his daughter, but not the first time Breanna had stood under his hard gaze. "You are basically interchangeable."

She would not flinch. It was not the first time he'd looked at them as one person split into two bodies. Not the first time their parents boasted a "two for the price of one" statement.

"King Sebastian did not indicate he cared which of you met him at the altar. It's not like we can tell you apart anyways."

Really selling this, Father.

"Breanna. No."

"I had picked out a different spouse for you, Breanna." Her father's gaze shifted to Annie. "A lesser title, but..." Lucas considered his daughters his possessions, objects to be bartered for his own goals.

A future marriage partner had never been discussed. No consultations with the potential bride. Not in this family. She was only still under this roof because Annie was terrified of what leaving meant.

"But that union is not available until his divorce is finalized next year. So..."

So Annie has a year. A year to get out.

She could help in the lead-up to the royal wedding…and figure out how to get herself out of this predicament, too. She had at least a year, right? It wasn't like royal weddings happened fast.

Her father shrugged; one daughter for another hardly mattered. The outcome was the same. "Ready for me to meet the king?"

Breanna needed to move. Needed to get the next part over with before she lost the burst of courage. She walked over to Annie, pulling her close.

"I love you. This has to be the last room."

Her sister squeezed her tighter than ever. "I love you."

Her arms were lead as she dropped them and pulled away. "Time to meet a king."

King Sebastian wasn't surprised to see the guard hovering by the door. The security on the Galanis estate rivaled the palace's. At least his guards were better at remaining unobtrusive.

This level of security felt more like they were keeping him in, rather than guarding. He had no intention of running. After all, he was here for a bride.

One that wanted to be a queen.

And this house held two such women. The Galanis family had not been quiet regarding the twins' plans to marry into a title. It was rumored no one was even considered a viable match unless they were at least a viscount.

Anastasia and Breanna Galanis were the only two who'd had a year's worth of entries in his brother's princess lottery. More than twenty-six thousand pounds had been spent between them for a chance at the title.

They'd walked away unhappy that day, but today Anastasia would become a queen.

Anastasia…the name he'd drawn out of a hat this morning.

It seemed somehow poetic that Sebastian had given his brother, Prince Alessio, so much grief for his bridal lottery. In fact, on the day he'd pulled Brie's name from the lottery, Sebastian had urged him to cancel the charade.

That charade had turned tourism around, reinvigorated the local economy, and most importantly, resulted in true love for Alessio and Brie. Sebastian was under no illusion that today's twist of fate would grant him happiness.

He thought he'd found love once. Samantha, a woman chosen for him by his father. Beautiful, educated, the perfect queen. His father had planned to make the announcement of their union. Then a stroke had rendered him unconscious for weeks, before finally claiming his life.

He and Samantha had bonded during that stressful time. Hiding their growing affection away from the prying lights of the media. He'd selfishly let his brother and his lotto bride take all the heat to protect the woman he loved.

And then the illusion shattered. Sam refused to understand why the crown was so heavy. She'd wanted it…desperately. Not him.

The same was true for his new bride-to-be, but at least he was under no illusions this time. With no expectations of happily-ever-after for Sebastian.

He was the king. King—the only thing anyone saw. Hell, the moment his father died, the staff at his bedside had called the time of death. Then turned and bowed to him.

Only in death was the power of the title vanquished. The title his father had served with every waking breath—just passed to another. A fate he'd had no part in choosing and no way to break.

Celiana's throne held little more than ceremonial power, but every poll in the last decade showed that the vast majority of the population wanted to maintain their monarchy. His people wanted a king. A head of state that didn't rotate out like the politicians. A constant in a world of chaos.

And the poll was worthless anyway. There was nothing in the country's constitution or laws that allowed for abolishment of the crown. He'd spent a year looking, devastation seeping in when the truth hit him. If Sebastian stepped aside, Alessio would be crowned.

And with Alessio happily married, the pressure

for marriage had been focused on him. Journalists, bloggers and random strangers hoped every woman he waved to or said hello to was his secret intended. One woman had fled the island after a photographer captured an innocent smile at a dinner outing. A simple interaction he couldn't recall the next day but that had altered her life forever.

Then a few weeks ago, he'd gone out for a stroll very early one morning, his guards at a close but not too close distance. A female jogger had raised her hand to him.

Someone had caught the interaction and uploaded it with sensational commentary that didn't match the moment. Social media had swiftly identified the single mother. It was like hounds descending on a target with no clue. It was cruel and unwarranted, and nothing he said seemed to make anyone listen.

At least after today those rumors would disappear.

He'd been raised to serve. This was what was expected of him. His and Anastasia's children would be next in line. But they'd know what was coming. Hopefully, he could find a way to prepare them better.

With time, he and Anastasia would become friends. That relationship had worked for his parents. Maybe not a great love, but peace in giving the kingdom the stability its residents craved was its own reward.

Wasn't it?

The door opened, and a striking young woman walked in. Brown curls falling to her shoulders. A blue dress custom-fit to her hips. Soft caramel eyes that looked him over with more than a hint of hesitation.

"Anastasia." He bowed. This wasn't the way one planned to meet a forever partner. Except it was in many aristocratic circles. Luckily, the Galanis twins had been trained since birth to expect this.

"I'm Breanna." She let out a soft sigh, then curtseyed. "Your Highness."

"Breanna?" He cleared his throat. "I—I…" There was no diplomatic way to ask why she was here instead of Anastasia.

"I am to be your bride." She didn't lift her head, and she didn't elaborate.

There was no script for this. "I asked for Anastasia."

"Why?" Breanna lifted her head, the caramel eyes catching his gaze. A few freckles dotted her nose.

She was gorgeous. Fierce. Challenging a king within moments of agreeing she was to meet him at the altar.

"Why?"

"That is what I asked. Why Annie?"

Sebastian shrugged. "You both had a full year's worth of entries in the bridal lottery."

"For Prince Alessio." Breanna clenched her fists, and her stance wavered for just a moment, but she didn't break eye contact.

Not for you.

The words were unstated, but they echoed in the room. The pinch of pain that brought was not to be acknowledged. Alessio was the fun one. The one who got to have a life…and love. The one who broke the rules. The one allowed to break the rules.

Most of his childhood he'd spent annoyed that Alessio refused to follow the rules. That he questioned the life they'd been brought up in. Part of him was probably jealous that his brother had choices—not many—but more than Sebastian.

Then Alessio had stepped in for him when he'd fallen apart after the crown landed on his head. The bond they should have had as brothers growing up finally solidified. Better late than never. He would not subject Alessio to the crown, or any woman who didn't want it.

Anastasia and Breanna had wanted it a year ago. And she wanted it enough now to switch places with the woman he'd asked for.

"I promise a queen's crown is far prettier." He leaned a little closer, hoping his smile looked convincing. The press was waiting. This was the only plan he had.

The deep brown eyes ignored the comment on the crown, and she crossed her arms, then looked to the door and uncrossed them. "You still haven't told me why you chose Annie."

"I pulled her name out of a hat."

Silence hung in the room for a moment before Breanna hugged her stomach and let out a chuckle that soon turned into a belly laugh. "A hat. A hat. Our lives decided by what you plucked from a hat. What if you'd pulled a rabbit out, Your Highness? Would a bunny have met you at the altar?"

She wiped a tear from her cheek, but the laughs continued.

He couldn't help it. His own chuckle combined with hers. "If I'd pulled out a rabbit, I would have been honor-bound to at least offer it the crown. Luckily for Anastasia, or I guess you, I didn't pull a rabbit."

Breanna's laughs died abruptly. "Right. Lucky for me."

The tilt of her lips was perfect. Just enough teeth showing for a believable smile, but there was something about it that sent a knife through his heart. "If Anastasia would rather…"

"I won the crown, Your Highness. Fair and square."

Won. The air in the room shifted on those three little letters. Won. He was a prize. Nothing more. The Galanis twins wanted titles; everyone knew that. And she was getting the top one.

As she straightened her shoulders, the brief

flash of pity, the question that maybe this was a misstep, disappeared. If Breanna wanted the crown more than Anastasia, then that was fine with him. Hopefully she wouldn't resent its weight too much after a few years.

"Your father was kind enough to let me use his office for a press conference. There are selected media there, and we will also broadcast the announcement of the engagement live."

"Now?" Breanna clutched her neck, a hint of pink creeping along it. "Press conference, now?"

"Yes. No time like the present. This is a marriage of convenience, after all. You get a crown. The country gets a queen. Everyone walks away happy."

Except me.

"And you get?" Breanna raised her brow, the challenge clear in her eyes.

If he believed in soulmates, he might get excited that it felt like she'd read his mind. Someone to share more than just the duty of it all. But wishing for love wouldn't make it appear. He was the king of Celiana. Nothing more.

"A partner to help me run Celiana." That was the truth. Most of it. He also got the press off his back and peace from constant rumors.

"Alessio and Brie love each other." Breanna swallowed, but she didn't break her gaze.

Another thing this union brought him. A way to crush the tiniest bit of hope that maybe he too could find love. That lightning could strike twice for the royal family of Celiana. But lightning wouldn't strike twice. He was the king. And this was his duty.

"They do. Which is good. Celiana has its royal love story. It doesn't need another."

"And what we need doesn't matter?" Breanna turned her head, her eyes widening as her father stepped into the room.

Lucas Galanis looked at his daughter, and his expression made Sebastian instinctively step closer to Breanna. He didn't touch her, but the urge to wrap an arm around her waist pulled at him. She was looking at her past, and he was her future. But he would not take an unwilling partner to the altar.

"If you do not want this—"

"Then Anastasia will be happy to meet King Sebastian at the altar." Her father didn't look at him. Some silent communication was seeping through the room.

This time he didn't hesitate. He wrapped an around her waist, surprised and pleased when she leaned into him.

"No. I am the choice. Not Annie." Breanna stepped out of his arms but pulled his hand into hers.

It was warm. Soft. A connection he wanted to lean into. Foolish dream, but at least they looked like a united front for the press. "Ready, Breanna?"

She didn't answer, but Lucas opened the door, and nodded to Sebastian—a far from friendly smile on his face. "After the royal couple." He bowed low, but somehow it felt almost mocking.

They started down the hall, her father a few steps in front of them. What was he supposed to say? What was the small talk etiquette of walking with your future bride less than ten minutes after you met her to announce a wedding? He'd had a lifetime of protocol training, and no one had covered this.

The buzz in the room was evident fifteen steps before they hit the door. The room was ready for whatever announcement was to come. Whether he and Breanna were was an irrelevant question.

He squeezed her hand as her father opened the door. Flashes of light hit them followed by a cacophony of questions. He'd promised them a statement, and the palace had said he would be taking no questions, but that didn't stop the determined lot from flinging them at the couple as he and Breanna stepped onto the podium.

"Good afternoon. I appreciate your patience as you waited for my bride and me." His fate… Breanna's fate…sealed in a single sentence.

The crowd seemed to lurch forward, and a wall of questions flooded them.

Sebastian raised a hand, the room quieting nearly instantly. "On Saturday, I will marry Breanna Galanis at the county offices at ten a.m.

This will be a small affair, like many of the weddings our people have. We will hold a reception after at the palace for close family and friends. As I know many of our citizens are currently struggling with inflation and the cost of living, the amount that would have been spent on the royal wedding will be divided evenly between Celiana's food banks, and local shelters that help the unhoused find affordable housing."

He took a deep breath. "Breanna and I look forward to many years together in service to Celiana. Thank you."

Sebastian raised his free hand, very aware that he was fast losing feeling in the hand Breanna had a death grip on. He walked them both through the door they'd entered and back to the room where they'd met.

"Saturday. We are getting married on Saturday? How?"

"You already have a dress, the one you wore at the lottery result. You will move into the palace with me tonight. We will do the minimal planning we need to. Start the process of getting to know each other, and then we will marry on Saturday."

"Oh, just like that. Right. Of course." The laughter escaping her throat was nearly manic.

"If you're having second thoughts…" He wasn't sure where he was going with that statement. After all, the announcement was made. They were marrying.

"No. I just wasn't planning to pack tonight." She balled her hands into fists and rocked on her heels. "So many things to put away."

That was an easy fix. Her father had ordered Anastasia's room packed up as soon as King Sebastian had arrived. The Galanis servants and the royal staff who'd traveled with him had certainly shifted the moment he'd learned it was Breanna who would be wearing the crown.

Given the efficiency of the team he'd brought, it was likely nearly done.

"My team started packing as soon as I arrived. I suspect most of the boxes are already loaded into the van. They are very good at their job."

"I'm sure they are." Breanna looked around the room, then nodded. "So, we get married."

Sebastian nodded, too. "We get married."

In three days.

CHAPTER TWO

THE ALARM'S INSULTING tone rocked the quiet room. Breanna reached for her phone, the shrill noise mocking the idea that she'd somehow found any rest after Sebastian showed her to her suite.

Between the exhaustion and brain fog following the announcement of their wedding, Breanna wasn't even sure of the path she'd taken to get here. She vaguely recalled something about him "fetching" her this morning. He'd probably even given her a time, but her brain hadn't absorbed the information.

Nope. All it knew was she was in the palace and marrying the king.

This weekend! How was this her life?

Her phone buzzed, the image of her sister popping up on the screen.

"Annie." Breanna sat up in bed, pushing her curls back. "Are you okay?"

That was one good thing. At least it was her in the palace. Not Annie. Their father hadn't won that round.

So why does it still feel like checkmate?

"I'm the one that should be asking that." Annie let out a soft cry. "Are you okay, Breanna?"

There was no good answer. She was dealing. That was probably the best she could manage. Particularly considering she didn't have a year to get out of this. Less than seventy-two hours stood between her and the throne.

"I'm handling it." Breanna sucked in a deep breath. "Now you."

"Not as well." She could picture Annie biting her lip on the other end of the phone, her eyes watering as she tried to sound brave for her twin. "Did they pack my portfolio in your boxes?"

Her portfolio.

My team started packing as soon as I arrived.

Sebastian had chosen Annie's name. They'd started packing up her sister's rooms. The portfolio she'd created. Their pathway out. Annie's pathway out.

It wasn't in Breanna's boxes. Because there were no boxes. Her room had been set up during her and Sebastian's dinner.

Breanna didn't remember any of the conversation. Maybe there hadn't been any. But when he deposited her at the door, she'd opened it to find the room exactly like hers at home, minus the cozy green walls Annie had chosen for her.

The laid-back beach house theme Annie selected was out of place against the royal ruby-red wall, but her bamboo chair was hanging from the ceiling. The houseplants she kept over her window were on the wire hanger she'd hung them from at home. The staff must have pulled it from the walls.

Even her sewing machine with the piece she'd been working on was set up in the corner of the room. The stitches not out of place at all. It was like her life had been picked up and moved across town.

Nothing to see here, just a complete change... and a wedding. Her chest tightened, but panicking was not going to do her any good.

The portfolio wasn't here. She was certain.

"Was your room tossed and messy?" She rubbed her free hand on her arm, trying to find some way to drive away the chill running through her. If the portfolio wasn't in Annie's room...if it was gone...

"No." Annie let out a sob. "I know they started packing, but they immediately stopped when you took my place. Everything is where it should be but the portfolio. I had it under my bed. The box it was in is there and empty."

Mother.

The woman was calculating. And she'd been conspicuously absent from the rest of the debacle with her daughters. A fact that was just now registering in Breanna's brain.

While their father was overseeing the announcement, she'd probably handled the packing. Going through their things. Recognizing that the hidden portfolio could only mean one thing.

"You need to leave, Annie." Her voice was strong. This had to happen now. Annie didn't have a year. Not if her parents considered her a flight risk. They had one soon-to-be-titled daughter, but two was better—at least to them.

"I can't. We will have less than nothing now. Without a portfolio, no one will employ me. And you as the former fiancée of…" Her sister's words died away, but Breanna could piece them together.

As the former fiancée of the king, no one would employ her either. They'd start from nothing. Less than nothing. Breanna might be willing to give it a go, but Annie wouldn't.

Her sister was the obedient first child. The one who never created waves. The one who bent and followed, even when it broke her spirit. Annie rarely said more than yes to her parents, hazarding a no only when she was sure that there'd be limited consequences.

To save her sister, there was only one choice.

Breanna looked around the room. Her room. Her forever. "And I am to be queen. So, you don't need our parents. You can redecorate the palace. Starting with my suite." She wasn't sure how to make that happen, but as queen, there had to be some perks, right?

"Breanna—"

"Leave, Annie. They can't come after the queen."

The queen. A marriage of convenience. There were worse situations. She'd never worry that her husband only wanted her because she was a Galanis.

She'd know forever that Sebastian hadn't plucked her name from a hat. She'd demanded the crown—and he'd decided she was good enough.

Story of her life. The second-born twin. The extra. The interchangeable bonus her parents got to use to their advantage.

The good news was it had trained to her to make the most of every bad situation. This was no different, and there were far worse situations to find yourself in.

Annie would get her dream. The one thing Breanna had always wanted was her sister's happiness. Annie's safety. And this was the best way to guarantee it.

She could be happy here. Or happy enough. It was all just a matter of mindset.

"Breanna."

"That's Queen Breanna to you." She giggled. It wasn't really funny. Or maybe it was. This was the universe's version of a joke. A pathetic one. But she'd make the most of it.

"Breanna…"

"I have a savings account. I started it years ago.

There is more than enough in it for a few months'
rental on a small apartment and some furniture.
Pack, Annie. Promise me. I will send you the
money as soon as you tell me you're gone."

"It's starting from nothing." Annie took a deep
breath. "Nothing."

"Not nothing. Those are Father's words. Words
designed to scare us. You are the sister of the
queen."

A pause hung over the line. She wanted to pull
the words out of her sister. But this had to be Annie's choice. Her decision. *Please.*

"You're right. Whatever is next has to be better
than whatever this is. It has to be." Her sister said
the final words more to herself than to Breanna.

Breanna looked at the ruby walls, so at odds
with her tastes. Annie was leaving. It wasn't the
way they'd planned, and they weren't together,
but Annie would be safe. And in a few years,
she'd be the country's top interior designer. Of
that Breanna had no doubt.

"I'll send you a text."

"Great." Breanna's breaths were coming fast
and hard, but hopefully her twin wouldn't hear
the panic pushing all around her. "And as soon as
you are a little settled, I need my room repainted.
It's red. Ruby. Very royal."

"And very too much." Annie giggled. "Laughter, is that a good sign or a bad one? This is too
much, Breanna."

It was. But they were on this path now. For better or worse. "Everything will be okay." Breanna said the words she always uttered when her sister was focused on the world falling apart.

"Or it won't." Annie let out her part of the phrase. "Those are the only two options."

"I choose." This was her choice. She was choosing Annie. "I am hanging up now. Pack and send me a text." Breanna swallowed the tears threatening. "I love you."

"Love you, too."

Then her sister was gone.

If she stood still, she'd give in to the wallow. The tears would flow, and she wouldn't be able to hold them back.

Walking into the suite next to her room, she looked at the overstuffed chairs and couch. Who would she host in here? No one.

"This is going to be my sewing room." Breanna put her hands on her hips, pretending this was a project that she wanted, rather than one forced upon her. Her twin was safe. Annie got her dreams. That was all that mattered.

The noises coming from the future queen's suite could be heard down the hallway. "What on earth is she doing?"

Away from the Galanis estate, Breanna had shut down. Whatever show she'd put on for the cameras had evaporated in private. He wasn't sure she even remembered the words he'd said on the ride to the palace. She'd sat through dinner, picking at the food, giving one- or two-word answers to everything.

The strong woman he'd met at the estate had wanted to be queen. The one across from him at dinner… He was less sure what this Breanna wanted.

She needed rest, and a good night's sleep. Sebastian had taken her to a suite not far from his. Technically the queen's quarters were connected to his, but his mother had never stayed in them.

His parents' relationship was one of cordial friendship, bound by respect. They'd done their duty with an heir and a spare. Put on a lovely show for the kingdom that made it appear they were ever so in love. In the palace, though, they'd lived separate lives.

Putting his soon-to-be wife in the queen's quarters felt like a step too far. And he'd already taken so many.

Standing at her door last night, he'd promised her that he'd pick her up today at nine, and they'd talk about next steps. If she was still in shock… Sebastian knew he'd offer her a way out. He wanted a willing queen. If she was having second thoughts, well, he'd cross that bridge when he had to.

He knocked, then opened the door to her suite.

Sebastian stopped, his hand on the door handle as his mouth fell open.

Most of the furniture was gone. There was still a small couch and an overstuffed chair that he didn't recognize. The rest of the suite now looked like a fabric store.

"What...?"

"Good morning, Your Highness." Breanna turned, her smile brighter than anything he'd seen yesterday. She looked happy. Ecstatic.

The perfect picture of a woman delighted to be in the palace. Good.

Her soft gaze held his. She was wearing what looking like old blue jeans and a flannel shirt, and her hair was pinned up in a polka-dot headscarf. Breanna was relaxed and busy.

And she was gorgeous.

"Good morning." He needed to say something else, but his mind seemed incapable of forming words.

Breanna tilted her head, then shrugged. "I hope you'd don't mind. But I figured I'd make this my sewing room. Give my bedroom a little more space."

"It's your suite." Sebastian cleared his throat. "I am glad the staff was directed to your sewing room." He'd given directions to make sure her room was packed and immediately unpacked. As little interruption to her life as possible.

There was already going to be so much change.

"I've never had a sewing room." Breanna crossed her arms, her eyes sparkling as they looked from the sewing machine in the corner to the cutting table in the center of the room.

Sebastian laughed. "Did you have a whole floor sewing suite? The palace is smaller than your estate, but there is plenty of room." If sewing made her happy, they'd clear all the space she wanted. Wearing the crown had some perks, after all.

Though he doubted she'd have a ton of free time for her hobby. A royal life was duty, meetings, events and then more duty.

"No, Your Highness."

"Sebastian. We are going to wed, after all." It was weird that moments ago he'd considered finding a way to grant her her freedom. But she'd been here less than twenty-four hours and was already redecorating. If she was happy to be queen, then he was content. Last night was simply overwhelming.

Understandable.

"Sebastian." Breanna hesitated for a moment. "Feels weird calling you Sebastian. Maybe after we've been married for a while."

"So, you didn't have a whole sewing floor? Was it more?" The Galanis compound could certainly hold more.

A small chuckle fell from her pink lips. "No, Sebastian." She tilted her head, like she was trying out his name for a second time. "I did not have a sewing room or a sewing floor or anything else. I had my room, which was large, but this—" she gestured to the craft table "—took up most of my free space."

There was more to that story. So much more. The way she parsed her words, weighing them. It was a strategy he recognized. One he'd used.

"I always assumed the Galanis twins would have their own palatial floors. To do with as they pleased. Any toy or hobby. Anything you chose."

Even a crown.

A curl slipped from her headscarf as she turned her attention to a yard of fabric. "You are the king, and before that you were the heir to the throne. Do you have a wing to do whatever you want with?"

There was something in her tone. A feeling of shared experience. A kindred spirit.

The Galanis twins were given the best of everything. Their parents' wealth granted access to places that were unimpressed by crowns. They were able to do anything they wanted.

And yet, neither had branched out from the family compound. Chosen their own path. They'd waited.

It had worked. She was to be a queen.

The thought cut him. She was getting a crown. That was worth holding out for…at least to some.

She placed a yard of fabric on a frame of some

type. "Did you have a wing for your favorite activity?"

"Kings don't have times for hobbies." It was a line his father had stated more than once when journalists asked what he liked to do when he wasn't performing a royal duty. It wasn't a lie either. King Cedric had never had a hobby.

He'd given everything to crown and country. That didn't leave much for anyone else.

"That is not true, Your—Sebastian." Breanna put her hands on her hips. The action was protective, and her pink lips were set in such a way it seemed she wanted to battle.

For me.

"You are allowed a hobby, Sebastian." She reached for his hand, squeezing it.

Her skin was fire, and he craved the heat. When she dropped his hand a moment later, ice flooded his system.

Control.

No one did battle for Sebastian. He had a role. A duty. And he played the cards he was dealt.

Played them well. His body went through the motions even during the year his heart had rebelled. But Breanna smelled so sweet. Like cinnamon, apples, and allspice. And the way she looked at him made him want to believe in fairy tales.

Mentally he pulled that intrusive thought from

his brain. It was just the hectic last couple of days. His heart refusing to fully accept what his mind already knew. This was a marriage of convenience between strangers.

She got a crown. He got a queen. Nothing more.

"I thought we should talk about our marriage. The union. The contract you signed for the princess lottery was a marriage contract. I had the lawyers look through it." They needed to discuss things other than hobbies. Or rather his lack of them. He woke early, worked until late, then repeated the process. That was all. Wishing for something different wouldn't bring changes. He knew his role.

"Lawyers. Right. I assume that means I've agreed to two children and my full participation in the royal family until I die. After all, there is no divorce in the Celiana royal family. Some ancient law no one wants to overturn." Breanna walked back to her sewing table and started laying pattern pieces over the garment.

"I remember the words I signed. My degree may be in early childhood education, but one does not grow up a Galanis without knowing some legalese." She repositioned the pattern pieces.

He wasn't sure she was really seeing the pieces, or maybe this was all part of the process.

"That is the general agreement. Yes."

"So, you are here to talk about the heir part or

the dutiful queen part?" She didn't stumble over the words. Said like they were nothing.

"The producing of an heir is part of the duty of a king and queen. An heir and a spare."

"No." Her curls bounced as she shot up. "No child of mine will be called a spare. Period. They are individuals. So, strike that word from your vocabulary, Your Highness."

Fire blazed in her dark eyes, and he nearly fell to his feet. He'd never been called a spare, but he knew the word had haunted his brother. The fact that Breanna was protective of their hypothetical children was the best sign he could think of.

"Consider it struck."

Her shoulders fell, and she bent over her table. He stepped beside her, rubbing her back. "Did you expect me to fight this?"

"Yes." Breanna stood, her body so close to his.

Emotions he hadn't let himself feel since his breakdown flooded his system. He wanted to laugh, to reach for her and bring out the chuckles he'd heard yesterday. Make her smile.

"I want my children to experience more than Alessio and I did. They deserve more."

"You do, too." Her hand brushed against his cheek.

The urge to lean into her, to say how much he hated the crown, was nearly overwhelming. But it wouldn't solve anything.

"We can conceive via IVF. The contract is for the marriage union, but you do not need to worry about sharing my bed." There were at least a dozen better ways to word that.

Breanna lowered her eyes and her hand dropped. "I see. Good to know."

"Breanna..."

A knock came, and his assistant stepped in before he could say anything else. A blessing since he had no idea what to say, and a curse given the tightening of her fists. At least one of the future queen's emotional tells was easy.

"Your Highness, Miss Galanis..." Raul bowed and then handed Sebastian a tablet. The bright words *Queen Bree!* radiated from the screen.

The headline was designed to draw attention to the similarities between Princess Briella and his Breanna. Briella and Alessio had an epic love story. The stuff of fairy tales.

And the exact opposite of this.

"Do you like the name Bree?"

"No." She stuck her tongue out, her nose scrunching as she shook her head.

So that was a definite no. They'd need to shut the press's nicknames down quickly. Once something stuck, it rarely unstuck.

"The press is likening you to Briella and the princess lottery."

"Princess Brie." Breanna cleared her throat.

"I guess our names and situations being similar makes this a natural association. I mean, they don't know you pulled my sister's name out of a hat rather than the glass bowl your brother used for his wife. However, I do not like the nickname. I have always been Breanna."

"This isn't the same. Alessio and Brie love each other." They cared for each other. To each other they were everything. The whole world. If Alessio lost his title tomorrow, Brie would still love him.

Sam had confirmed what his father always said. Sebastian, without the crown, was nothing. Without the title, he had no place in this world. Everything about him revolved around a position he'd done nothing to earn.

"They didn't when he pulled her name from the glass bowl." Breanna tapped on the screen, making the text easier to read. "Looks like people enjoy your small wedding idea."

Shifting the topic was good. What was there to say? Neither expected the same to happen for them. "It makes a good statement. Makes us seem more regular when others have lost much in the last few years." The words felt off.

He wanted to acknowledge that many in the island nation were still suffering from the economic downturn. But the idea of having a giant celebration for such a union was unsavory. This was duty. Partnership. To spend Celiana's funds on such a thing would be unfair to the citizens.

"Royals caring. Always a good public relations call." Breanna stuck her hands in her pockets and rocked backwards. "So, umm… I don't think you just wanted to show us this." She paused. "Sorry, I don't think we've been introduced."

"Raul, my lady. The king's personal assistant." Raul bowed his head and held out his hand for the tablet. Once he had it, he tapped out several commands. "I wanted to go over a few things for the wedding. We got a list of your likes from your parents, but just checking. You want a bouquet of daisies and sunflowers?"

Breanna started to roll her eyes, then seemed to catch herself. "Only if you want me to sniff all the way down the aisle. Is there an aisle at the magistrate's? Or is it just a hallway?"

She shook her head. "Not the point. Focus, Breanna."

"Nice to know I am not the only one who talks to myself." Sebastian winked, wanting to overcome the negative feelings his early comments must have caused.

"A hard habit to break." Some of the tension leaked from her shoulders as she looked at him. "I am allergic to those. My parents tend to forget that Annie and I aren't exactly interchangeable. I am allergic to flowers; she can't get stung by bees. Anyways, I tolerate hydrangeas."

Interchangeable? They were identical in looks but still two different people. He couldn't focus on that now, though.

"Tolerate?" Sebastian shook his head. "No." She was marrying a stranger. The least he could do was give her flowers that didn't make her nose itch. "What flower can you be around easily?"

"Define *easily*." She looked at her feet, a hint of pink tracing her chin. "I can do ferns and pothos. I keep those in my room, but they aren't exactly royal wedding bouquet material."

Ferns and pothos. He knew the first. The second…surely a florist could figure something out?

"It's fine. It's not like I have to carry the bouquet for long. I can make do."

Make do. Words he was so familiar with. His whole life was concessions. Hers was now, too. Flowers for her bouquet were a choice that could be all hers.

"What about succulents?" Sebastian remembered seeing a beautiful design when Brie and Alessio were planning their union. Brie went with bright flowers for her bouquet, but the succulent option was stunning.

"Succulents? I mean, sure. I can also do cacti… they each have about the same amount of pollen. As close to zero as possible."

"Succulent bouquets are a thing. So, let's do that. Cacti would be a unique choice, but a little too prickly." Sebastian pointed to the tablet, happy when Raul picked up his cue to search for bouquet images. "Imagine the headlines if you carried cacti."

"Prickly queen! Touchy!" Her giggle was good, but those were just a few of the things the press might say.

He took the tablet and moved closer to her. She stepped closer, too. Not touching, but close. If this were a real relationship, he could put an arm around her. Instead, he swiped, showing off the different online options, watching her closely to see if any sparked her interest.

Breanna grabbed his hand as a small bouquet caught her eye. Her finger wrapped around his for an instant before she pulled back and cleared her throat. "These are pretty; let's do that."

Had she meant to touch him? Had she wanted more? Questions there was no easy way to ask a stranger, particularly in company.

"Anything else we should know?" Raul was poised, ready to take down any details.

Breanna seemed to purposefully step away from him. "I don't eat meat, and am not a huge fan of chocolate. Other than that, I am pretty easygoing. Promise."

"So, the steak and chocolate cake need to be canceled, too." Raul looked to Sebastian, the condemnation of her parents clear in his face.

Sebastian felt the same. This was not a traditional union, but Breanna deserved to make her own choices. "How about we go over everything and choose for ourselves?"

Breanna's shoulders relaxed, and she started to lean towards him before catching herself. "Thank you."

CHAPTER THREE

"YOU CAN STILL end this. You do not have to do this."

"I seem to remember saying something along the same lines, brother. You still pulled Brie's name out of the crystal bowl you made. It worked out." Sebastian didn't expect love for himself and Breanna. But they got along well enough, and she wanted the crown. This would be fine.

He straightened his tie for the hundredth time. "Why won't this damn tie stay where I put it?"

"Because you keep pulling at it." Alessio crossed his arms and looked towards the door, probably hoping that his wife, Brie, would make an appearance.

"Brie is with Breanna. She isn't going to come in here. It's royal custom for the princess to attend to the queen-to-be." Sebastian said the words with more conviction than he felt. He wasn't at all certain that Princess Brie would adhere to custom.

And it wouldn't be the worst thing if his sister-in-law arrived. Alessio could use the princess's calming effect. Though knowing Brie, she would have far more to say about today than his brother.

Alessio stalked to the mirror, pushing Sebastian's hands away from his tie. "Nothing about this is custom." His brother straightened the tie, then grabbed Sebastian's hands and pushed them into his pockets.

"Don't touch it!"

Sebastian wanted to pull his hands from his pockets on principle, but the tie was finally straight. "I think most of this actually is custom. I am just being honest about it. The fairy-tale stuff? The romance of royal unions—well, with present company excluded—we both know what it's really like."

"You can have more." Alessio threw his hands up, reaching for his own tie. "You deserve more. Just because you are the king. Sebastian—"

"Careful not to mess your tie." It was a pathetic joke, but what else was he supposed to say? Alessio got lucky.

Jealousy was pointless. He was genuinely happy for his brother. Brie was his match. But wanting it for himself wouldn't make it happen.

He was the king. That was all he was to almost everyone. Sure, his brother saw a different version, but the kingdom...even his own mother... saw only the crown.

The year he'd rebelled, he'd caused so much grief for Alessio. The fact that his brother had handled it perfectly didn't matter. Alessio had saved the kingdom. His and Brie's lottery had turned everything around. They deserved the happily-ever-after.

But Alessio should never have been put in that position. Sebastian had been raised for this role; he should have accepted it right away.

The frustration on his brother's face made it clear that Alessio had far more to add to this conversation. "Sebast—"

A knock echoed through the room, interrupting Alessio's next attempt. "Saved by the bell… or knock." He winked at his brother before walking over to the door. Sebastian pulled it open with flair, then stood there, not sure what to say.

Breanna was dressed in a floor-length white gown. The mermaid cut hugged her in all the right places. The scalloped top accentuated the swell of her breasts. Her dark hair was loose, curls wrapping her beautiful features, and her makeup looked natural. It was like she'd stepped from the pages of a bridal magazine.

In a few hours, she'd be his queen.

"Breanna."

"Well, hell." She crossed her arms, then looked around him and waved at Alessio. "Your wife was right, he's not in a tux."

"Umm…" Sebastian looked at his suit and waited for his brain to find any kind of statement. It was an afternoon wedding. At the magistrate's.

A tux seemed out of place, but if she wanted him dressed in one, he had multiple.

Breanna hitched up her train and nodded to the interior. "Can I come in?"

"Isn't there a superstition about the groom seeing the bride in her dress before the wedding?" Sebastian wanted to reel the words back in as Breanna's face fell.

The hurt vanished in a flash. She shrugged and moved past him. "I think that curse only applies to those who aren't marrying out of duty."

Alessio made a noise and then started for the door. "I'll give you two a minute."

"No." Breanna held up a hand. "Brie said you should stay for this part."

This part?

His brother halted by the door. If Brie told him to stay, even through an intermediary, he'd do it. Until whatever *this part* was concluded.

"You are in a day suit. A lovely one. You're very attractive." A delicate rose coated her cheeks.

"I mean, you look nice. The suit. The suit looks nice." Breanna cleared her throat. "Wow. There really is no playbook for confronting the stranger you are marrying."

"Maybe we can write one." Sebastian playfully stroked his chin, trying to make his bride smile. *"No Big Life Decisions: Marrying a King in Three Days or Less."*

She tilted her head, "We need to workshop the title."

"Sure." Sebastian stuffed his hands in his pockets. "While we think of better titles, what is the problem with my suit?"

"I am in *this*." She frowned as she looked down at the exquisite gown, her fingers rustling over the beaded top.

"You look lovely." Such an understatement. Breanna sparkled as the light hit the jewels hand-sewn over the intricate gown.

"That is one of Ophelia's gowns, is it not? An original?" Sebastian knew most of the women from the princess lottery had rented their dresses. But the Galanis twins' gowns were specially made. With a year's worth of entries, the identical twins stood front and center as the odds of Alessio pulling out their names was high.

The twins were the focus of most of the early images on the day of the lottery, their bright, fancy dresses plastered everywhere. Commentators had discussed how their dresses even matched each other as Alessio drew the name, but he couldn't remember anyone saying if they looked upset not to hear their names.

"Yes. My and Annie's dresses were the most expensive gowns Ophelia has ever made."

"The price hardly matters." He doubted the price tag, even for two wedding dresses, had made a dent in the Galanis fortune.

"Except it does. People will talk." Breanna shook her head. "It is too fancy for this. Particularly with you dressed that way. The Galanis family upstaging the king."

The headline practically wrote itself.

"You want me to change?" He pointed to his closet. "My wardrobe is yours. Whatever you choose, I will put on. I have several tuxes." They weren't his first choice, but if that was what she chose, he'd put it on with a smile. "We can toss this offending day suit back in the depths where it belongs."

Breanna took a deep breath, her face softening. "You're very handsome, and the suit is lovely—as I said."

As compliments went, it was a tiny one. But coming from Breanna's sweet lips, it felt like he'd won a prize. "Handsome." He struck a pose, enjoying the giggle she let slip out.

She snapped her fingers. "Focus. This isn't the first time you've been told you're handsome."

"My future wife saying it feels different." He meant it. He didn't know why it made his insides gooey, but it did.

Breanna raised an eyebrow but didn't add anything else to that conversation. Instead, she pointed to her gown again.

"I can't wear this dress." Breanna took a deep breath. "We are having a small wedding. One similar to regular people, right?"

"Yes." Sebastian looked to Alessio, who'd remained painfully quiet during this exchange. But if his brother understood the issue, he wasn't giving anything away. Instead, he was looking at Breanna, a smile pulling at the corner of his lips. "I thought, given the cost of living crisis, smaller is better."

"Right. And this dress cost more than fifteen thousand pounds." Breanna sighed. "That is not a good look for that message, Your Highness."

He didn't like how the exasperated "Your Highness" fell from her lips.

"Breanna..."

She looked at the crystals lining the bodice. "I know you picked my name, or rather Annie's, because we had a dress, but this won't work."

What was the answer? They were heading to the magistrate's office in less than two hours. But she was right. If the cost leaked, and it would, the public relations team would be dealing with a nightmare.

"Do you have a plan to solve the issue?" Alessio had asked the right question. The one that should have popped from his mouth minutes ago.

Sebastian looked to Breanna, and nodded, hoping she had an idea.

"I have a dress. It's white—mostly. I made it from a dress I found at a thrift store a few years ago. It's simple, and I think it is the better choice. But if *you* want this..."

She had a simple gown. One she'd made. It wasn't exactly what people thought of when they imagined a royal wedding.

Though what about this was?

Breanna waited, then turned to Alessio. "Do you think I'm wrong?"

"No. And let me guess, Brie agrees with you." Alessio looked at his watch. "Brie's pretty good at estimating the press's response."

His fiancée's smile wasn't forced when Alessio mentioned his wife. Breanna sparkled, and it had nothing to do with the fancy dress. "She does. The princess is very kind."

"She is." Alessio nodded. "Do you need anything else from me?"

"No." Breanna shook her head, "You're free to go."

"Dismissed by the queen." Alessio bowed to the queen. This his gaze focused on Sebastian. "I like her." Then he was gone.

Sebastian had said the same thing about Brie to Alessio.

"Nothing about this is standard, but I figured you chose a couture gown for the lottery, and you won't get to wear it again." There was a law in place that kept the king and queen from divorcing. An ancient crusty script from a bygone era that parliament had never overruled.

The lyrical notes of her chuckle made him smile.

"I hate this dress. I didn't choose it. Mother did." She reached for his hands, then pulled back.

Mother did.

The words stuck in his head. That wasn't right. Breanna and Anastasia wanted titles. Everyone knew that. The press had followed their journeys for the princess lottery nearly as closely as they'd followed Alessio. A look inside the day of royal hopefuls.

Only after Briella's name bounced out did the Galanis twins' names fade from the press.

She wanted this. *But what if...*

"There was something else I wanted..." She looked at her feet, then straightened. "Kiss me." Breanna let out a nervous sound. "Wow, I probably could have stated that differently. Or maybe not at all, but too late now, so, yeah. We'll go with that. I want you to kiss me."

Her dark eyes flitted to the door, and color crept along her neck. "Breanna?" Kissing her wouldn't be hard. The woman was the definition of beauty. But her nervousness gave him pause.

"Have you ever kissed anyone?" The twins were waiting for a title, but surely she'd dated. She must have had suitors lined up around the family compound.

"Nope." Breanna bit her lip and let out a ragged breath. "I—I—I need to say something other than *I*, but my brain is overloaded."

Sebastian took her hand; the connection was

firm but loose enough that if she wanted to pull back, it would take no effort. He was thrilled when she didn't. "Do you trust me?"

"I should say no. That is what makes sense."

Once more his soon-to-be bride was right. They were practically strangers, but he felt an odd sense of calm right now. Nerves should be popping; he should be fidgeting, but the only thing weighing on him was how to make this moment special for her.

"I trust you." She bit her lip, again. "Today is a lot, but I trust you. I do. Guess I am practicing for the vows." Her soft smile warmed his heart. "I do."

The phrase seemed to unlock part of his soul. The words were sustenance on this day where everything felt more than a little surreal.

Using his free hand, he stroked her lip, pulling it from her teeth. "You are safe here." *With me.*

Yes, they were marrying. But he was not going to force anything on Breanna. They'd get to know each other. Learn to coexist and care for each other. It would take time, but she was safe. Always.

"Close your eyes." The words were barely above a whisper, but she did as he said.

A person only got one first kiss. Usually, it was fumbling and more than a little off as teens in the heady days of hormones figured out what the racing feelings meant. That was not the experience Breanna was going to get. But he could still make it memorable.

He squeezed her hand, trying to push as much reassurance through the touch as possible. "Breathe, honey." Sebastian let his free hand stroke her cheek.

Fire danced on the tips of his fingers. This was about Breanna. Giving her a memory. Still, his breath was picking up, and desire seemed to pulse on each breath.

Breanna.

So much of his life was out of his control. Even the woman before him wasn't his choice. But in this moment, it felt like the universe was granting something just for him.

"Sebastian."

His name. Just his name. Not his title, nothing else, fell from her sweet lips.

Finally, he pressed his lips to hers. He'd envisioned a short, nearly chaste kiss. A memory given to her, enjoyed by him.

Instead, the universe exploded. Breanna leaned into him, and his arms went around her waist without another thought, her hands wrapping around his neck.

Apples, lemons, sweetness divine filled his nostrils as his soon-to-be wife's body fit against his. Time, space and everything in between vanished as he drank her in.

Then her mouth opened, and the taste of her

nearly brought him to his knees. If the afterlife contained a paradise, the feeling of Breanna in his arms, lips pressed to his, would be the ultimate achievement possible.

"You cannot possibly wear that." Breanna's mother never raised her voice, but her tone right now was as close to hysterical as she could remember. "Your little hobby is cute when it is contained at home. But this is your wedding day. To the king."

"As though you wouldn't know what today is or who you are marrying." Princess Brie laughed and held up the champagne goblet. Her bright blue eyes sparkled as she met Breanna's gaze. "You are gorgeous."

Brie was saying all the things Breanna wanted to say to her parents but without a hint of bile or anger. Yet the daggers found purchase each time. The princess had skillfully put her mother in her place over and over again without ever raising her voice or getting testy. She was poised, confident and so sure that what she said would have the exact response she intended.

This was why Brie had broken from her powerful family. Started her own business. Created a name for herself. Even after marrying a prince, the patriarch and matriarch of the Alessio clan still didn't acknowledge the daughter, who outshone them all.

It was that willingness to take a leap that led Brie to carving her own path, while Breanna had made plans. But never followed through. Sure, she'd protected Annie, but she was still marrying a king she didn't know in less than an hour.

Sebastian. His name cascaded through her mind. Her hand reflexively found her lips where the ghost of the kiss remained.

Maybe first kisses were always like that. Maybe your body felt like singing each time. It wasn't like she'd had any experience with it.

The boy she'd fancied at uni had stood her up for their first date. Later, she'd heard through the rumor mill that her father had paid the man quite handsomely to forget she existed. Whether it was true or not, and she suspected it was, all the men who'd asked her out afterwards seemed to be hoping they might also get the same fat check.

Life as a Galanis was privileged in many ways…but it did not come with freedom.

She hadn't expected his lips to feel so soft, so sweet, so refreshing. Kissing Sebastian felt like taking a sip from a fresh stream. Her body had nearly collapsed with want and need.

She'd pressed herself against him, lengthening the exchange. Desperate for another.

Focus!

Annie's hand pressed into hers, grounding her.

"I think she looks beautiful." Her sister cleared her throat, then continued, "That dress is gorgeous and looks nothing like the original dress you bought."

Her sister made a face. "It was hideous. I thought there was no way you could make it anything."

"I've thought that about your room ideas, too." Breanna pulled her sister close.

"You both have far too much faith in your abilities."

Annie straightened her shoulders, then looked at her mother. A week ago, those sharpened words would have bowed her spirit. Instead, she shrugged and twirled a finger through the curl by her cheek.

It was the only thing Matilda Galanis had said to Annie, and it was clear she wanted Annie to respond. Good for Annie that she was rewarding her mother with the same indifference she'd shown her.

The Galanis Trust had made it known that Annie was not under their protection, and she'd been cut off. Which meant renting an apartment had been nearly impossible.

The only one they'd found was in a neighborhood people did their best to avoid. But the price was right, and the landlord had been willing to rent it on a month-by-month basis.

Breanna could have asked Sebastian for aid. But Annie had begged her not to. She claimed she'd needed to do as much of this on her own as possible. Breanna hadn't wanted to steal away any of her newfound confidence.

Breanna squeezed Annie's hand, then examined herself in the floor-length mirror. The dress was a vintage wedding gown she'd found at a local thrift store. The bottom had been stained, so Breanna cut it off, making this a tea-length gown. She'd added a crochet-like overlay, giving it a semiformal look. It was pretty, and handmade. It hung on her perfectly.

If she'd had a choice in the dresses she was allowed to pick for the princess lottery, she'd have chosen something like this. Light. Airy.

It didn't scream queen attire. Her mother was right about that. But it was perfect for her.

The sounds of the square's bell ringing echoed in the room. Time to go. Annie stepped to her side and kissed her cheek.

"You don't have to do this." Her sister's words were nearly silent, but the plea under them echoed into the universe.

Breanna put her hand on her sister's cheek. If she didn't there'd be no way for them to get Annie back up on her feet. Not for years…if ever. Her sister had goals and a plan, and the soon-to-be queen could protect her better than she'd ever hoped for. "I know."

Then she looked at her mother and Princess Briella. "I think that ringing is the sign that we are supposed to head to the magistrate's office."

She'd not fumbled a single word. Pride and worry raced for first place in her mind.

Now, if I can manage not to stumble over my vows.

"You all right?" Sebastian's hand slid around her waist as she stood at the corner of the reception area. It was a light afternoon affair. Finger sandwiches, fruit, and for dessert, her favorite, lemon cake. It might be a normal reception. Except they were in the palace.

And a small gold crown was pinned to the top of her hair.

What a day. She started to lean into him, then pulled herself upright. He was her husband, checking on her. But they were still virtually strangers.

"Fine." The lie was easier than the truth. And it had nothing to do with the small crown Sebastian had placed on her head after she'd said *I do.*

No. Once more in her life, the upset was caused by the people who'd raised her. Or at least paid for the host of rotating nannies she and Annie loved and lost in their childhood.

Nothing about the day was right for them. The dress. The location. And now the reception.

They'd expected a huge party. Despite the press conference clearly outlining the fact that they were having a simple reception for close friends and family, they'd expected palace glamour. They'd wanted a queen for a daughter…but only if they could flash it to the world.

"This might as well be a pauper's reception. Where is the steak?" Her father's complaint carried across the room, and most of the heads turned in his direction.

Breanna started towards him, grateful that Sebastian moved with her.

"It's an afternoon reception, father." Breanna kept her voice low, hoping he might do the same.

Lucas Galanis got what he wanted. On the few occasions he didn't, hell tended to spill from its gates.

"Cucumber sandwiches, carrot and raisin sandwiches? It's positively ghastly." Her mother huffed as she looked at the fare on her plate.

"There is smoked salmon, too." Breanna was a vegetarian. It was something she'd adopted after watching an online video when she was a teenager. Her father had called it a phase. A decade later, "the phase" was still intact. It infuriated him.

"And lemon cake," Sebastian offered, squeezing her side.

She'd never had anyone stand next to her while she tried to calm her parents. Annie had always avoided conflict.

Then she looked at her husband and felt her head snap back a bit. His eyes were boring into her father's. Fury matching her father's radiated in her husband's gaze.

Over what?

"Lemon cake." Her mother sniffed.

Sebastian's hand tightened on her waist.

Without thinking, she put her hand around his waist. They were a united front.

"Yes. Lemon cake." Sebastian's words were ice spikes, but neither of her parents appeared to pick up on the cool tones. "*Breanna's* favorite." The world seemed to shift, and the pressure on her chest evaporated. He was here. Choosing her side. Choosing Breanna. No one ever chose her.

Her mother let out a soft chuckle. "Chocolate is what *we* ordered."

Ordered. Like today was theirs. Their accomplishment. Their achievement. Not an irreversible life-changing moment for their daughter.

Before she could say anything, Sebastian offered, "It's *her* wedding day."

Her day. Hers. Such a simple statement that rocked her world. She leaned her head against his shoulder, enjoying having a partner for this exchange.

His lips brushed the top of her head, and she saw her mother's eyes narrow. They really didn't care if their daughter was happy. Maybe they didn't want that.

"Yes. But *we* are the ones that wanted to be here. Breanna didn't want the crown—" Her father looked at Sebastian, keeping his head tilted just enough for the king.

"Father—"

"He needs us, Breanna." He cut her off. "The country is a constitutional monarchy. They have no real power. He showed up on our doorstep for a bride, and we provided one."

And yet you wanted a daughter to wear the crown.

"Breanna, do you want your parents here?"

The soft question nearly made her laugh. Want her parents here? Of course not. She never wanted her parents around, but they were her parents.

Sending them away wasn't an option. Or it hadn't been before Sebastian put a crown on her head. "No?"

She hadn't really meant to say it as a question. It felt rebellious. Far more rebellious than anything else she'd ever done.

And liberating.

"Lovely. My wife, *your queen*, and I bid you farewell." Sebastian nodded towards the door. "Don't make me call the guard. In this palace, my word is final."

"Breanna, you don't mean to let him send us away." Her mother stepped towards her, but Breanna stepped back. Sebastian moved with her in unison.

"Where is Annie's portfolio?" It wasn't the answer to her mother's question, but Matilda Galanis was a smart woman. She knew the underlying question.

Her mother's eyes flitted to Annie, currently laughing with Prince Alessio and Princess Briella. She looked to her husband, then shrugged. "What portfolio?"

The lie was too much. Her mother knew what she meant. If the portfolio hadn't been burned, then it had been locked away. It didn't matter. The result was the same.

"Have a nice day." Breanna nodded to her parents, then turned attention to Sebastian. "Shall we dance?" A DJ had been quietly playing tunes, but no one had ventured onto the dance floor.

"Is that what you want?" Sebastian's gaze followed her parents' exit, then refocused on her.

No one, other than Annie, had ever asked her what she wanted. She was light. Happy. And she wanted to enjoy the moment.

"Yes. Let's dance!" She grabbed her husband's hand, trying to pretend that the king hadn't just kicked her parents out of their wedding reception. That this was just a fun afternoon get-together. The illusion would clear when Annie, Alessio and Brie all left. But until she was left alone with Sebastian—in the palace—Breanna could try to forget that she'd said *I do* to a king today.

A king. And a stranger.

Breanna hit her hip against his as the music bounced around them. His bride had kicked her shoes off five songs ago. Brie and Annie had followed suit. Only his mother still had her shoes on.

The dowager queen would leave her shoes on even if her toes were bleeding. But at least his mother was smiling. She'd even discreetly given him a thumbs-up when he'd told Breanna's parents to leave.

The fast song shifted to a slow tune. Briella and Alessio immediately went into each other's arms. A few other couples did the same while some of the singles exited the dance floor.

His wife stood still; her jeweled gaze watched him closely. Should he reach for her? They were married, but the fast dances let them be close without holding each other.

Did she want to dance in his arms? She'd put her arm around his when he was kicking her parents out. He'd kissed the top of her head, unable to resist. Breanna has pulled him onto the dance floor, but she hadn't touched him other than hip bumps and the occasional high-five since. And much of the dancing was in groups.

He was never more than a few inches from her. If she moved, he moved with her. And she'd done the same. He wanted to pull her close, hold her, but the day was already so much. They were husband and wife, but in title only.

The chords twanged on, and Breanna cleared her throat. "I am going to get a drink." She dipped her head to him, her eyes shielded.

Make a decision, Sebastian!

"I'll come with you."

Breanna nodded as she moved off the dance floor. There was nothing different in her posture, but he knew he'd hurt her feelings. It wasn't his intent, but the outcome was the same.

"Breanna." He said her name without knowing where he was going next. "Did you want to dance?"

"We've been dancing." His wife touched the crown he'd placed on her head after they'd said *I do*. "Your mother pinned this in perfectly. It hasn't moved with all the motion. She'll have to teach me how to do that."

"I am sure she'd be happy to." Sebastian grabbed two lemon drop mocktails, handed one to his wife and sipped his. The sugar on the rim blended with the tartness, but it didn't cut any of the awkwardness hovering between them now as they stood silently drinking the festive beverage.

The ease they'd had bouncing to the rhythms on the floor had evaporated. He wanted it back.

The slow song stopped, but the couples on the dance floor clung to each other for several moments after the final chords echoed. At most weddings, the bride and groom were center-stage.

But this wasn't a traditional reception in any sense of the word, and the couples staring at each other with love were not the bride and groom.

His eyes again went to Alessio and Brie. They were whispering to each other as they moved to a beat no one else heard. No doubt saying the sweet nothings those in love spoke so easily. He looked to Breanna and barely caught the sigh in his throat.

A fast song kicked in. Good. They could get back on the dance floor.

"Breanna!" Brie bounced towards her sister-in-law. "This one is just for the girls." The princess stole the queen into the center of the floor with a host of giggles.

"Why did you stand there when your bride was looking at you, waiting for you to ask her to dance?" His mother's voice was quiet, but it carried an authority that made his back a little straighter.

The dowager queen looked at the dance floor. Her eyes rested on the queen and princess. "She wanted to dance with you. She is your wife."

"I froze." Sebastian finished the last of his drink. There was no use calling it anything else. The day was one for the record books. He was married to a woman whose parents insinuated she hadn't wanted the crown he'd thought she craved. It was enough to throw anyone off their game.

"Breanna wants you to show her how you pinned the crown so well. It hasn't moved." It was a bad segue but easier than anything else.

His mother sniffed but didn't offer anything

else on that topic. "You will dance with her the next time a slow song comes on. Brie bought you a few minutes."

"Wha...?" He turned to see and caught Alessio's eyes as he waved to him from where he stood next to the DJ stand.

"He's helping you." His mother patted his arm. "He wants you and your queen to be happy."

"Do you think we can be?" He regretted the words as soon as they were out.

His mother looked to the dance floor again. "Happiness is much to ask for in a royal marriage. Contentedness. Maybe that will be in your reach."

Contentedness.

Was that what she and his father had had? Contentedness. Was that enough?

It would have to be.

The slow song began, and Alessio collected his wife. Sebastian started for the dance floor and met Breanna at the edge of it.

"May I have this dance?"

She looked over her shoulder, her eye following Alessio and Brie's rotations on the floor. Then she reached for his hand and squeezed it. "Only if you actually want it."

Of course his bride knew this wasn't by chance.

Not dropping her hand, he pulled her onto the dance floor and into his arms. "I very much do."

She slid her arms around his waist, gently

swaying with him on the floor. After a moment she laid her head against his shoulder.

He breathed her in, holding her tight. Enjoying the moment a little too much.

"It's been a day." The whispered words were so soft he wasn't sure she'd meant to say them out loud.

His fingers stroked her back, and she melted against him a little more. They weren't so much dancing as holding on to each other as the storm of the day finally broke.

It didn't matter. They were together. Day one of a lifetime.

"We made it through the reception." She chuckled, "And our first family drama."

They had.

"What's next, Sebastian?"

"Next?" He looked over his shoulder at his mother, holding mini court with a few friends. She missed his father, but if he were still here, they would have stood near each other but never danced together. Two people who cared for each other but did not have a deep passion.

Two strangers who'd married.

Then his gaze fell on Brie and Alessio. They were holding each other, talking quietly, and laughing at a private joke. Two strangers who'd fallen desperately in love. A lightning strike.

Looking away brought more peace than it should. His brother and sister-in-law were happy.

"We get to know each other." He smiled at his bride, seeing the uncertainty in her gaze. He and Breanna would be content. It would be enough.

It had to be.

CHAPTER FOUR

SEBASTIAN DOWNED THE cup of coffee, then poured himself another. He and Breanna had danced for hours last night. His legs burned with the memory of the exercise. But it was his heart that had kept him awake all night.

She'd held him tight through their final slow dance. Knowing the reception was nearly over. Today began the real story. Their life as king and queen.

But we are the ones who wanted to be here.

Her parents' words kept replaying in his mind. That couldn't be right. Breanna had won the crown from her sister. She'd wanted it more.

I think that curse only applies to those who aren't marrying out of duty.

So many phrases were burned into his brain from yesterday. As was the feel of her body against his. The soft scent of cinnamon apples in her hair seemed attached to his nose. Her downcast eyes as she'd quietly said I do in the magistrate's office.

The brush of her lips on his.

So many emotions to work through before the day had really even begun.

"I do hope you haven't drunk all the coffee." Breanna's voice was bright. No dark circles shadowed her eyes. She looked well-rested.

His mind couldn't seem to align the words her parents had thrown at him yesterday and the bubbly woman pouring her own cup of coffee beside him.

"Not to complain, but is there any coffee syrup hiding anywhere?" Breanna looked to the cabinets like she was considering opening them but holding back.

"Not in this kitchen." Sebastian pulled up his phone, ready to text her order to the staff. The fact that she hadn't asked for syrup when she first arrived was frustrating. But she was asking now. "What do you want?"

"This kitchen? So how many kitchens are there?" Breanna went to the fridge, found some milk, poured it in, and then added more sugar than he'd ever seen someone put in such a small cup.

"Several." Take Breanna on a tour of the palace…today's task. "This is my, *our*, private kitchen. There isn't staff for this one, but it's always stocked with what I—we—want. I just need to know what that is."

"Do you cook?" Breanna slid onto one of the high stools.

"Yes, when I have time." Sebastian took a deep breath because part of him wanted to shake the phone in her face and demand the answer to the question he'd asked and she'd now dodged several times.

"What syrups do you like, Breanna?"

"It's no big deal." Breanna put her elbows on the counter, then rested her chin in her hands. It was adorable and infuriating at the same time. "So, what do you like to cook? Eggs? I swear that is what the movies always show. The man makes the girl scrambled eggs in the morning and everyone swoons—he can cook."

"I will answer that question when you tell me what syrups you want stocked in here. If you don't tell me, then I will have the staff order one of everything."

She laughed and gestured to the kitchen. "This kitchen is huge, and I still don't think you could fit one of everything."

"I guess we get to see then." Sebastian started typing.

Her hands were warm as they wrapped around his wrist. "It's not a big deal, Sebastian. And its early. Don't disturb the staff on my behalf, please."

Tears hovered in her eyes. "Please."

He set the phone down and walked to her without thinking of the next steps. Sebastian pulled her into his arms. She was still sitting on the stool, and her head barely came to his shoulder. "It's coffee syrup, Breanna. It's not earth-shattering, but it's something you want, so I will put in the order this afternoon. You will have it tomorrow."

She nodded against him and sniffed. "This is silly. I don't know why syrup is sending so many emotions through me."

It wasn't syrup. It was everything else coming through something that didn't matter in the universe's grand scheme. He'd had similar breakdowns when the crown got too heavy. Worrying over something minor was easier than addressing the elephant in the room.

"A lot has happened in four days." That was an understatement. He stroked her back, then leaned his head against hers.

No words. Just two people who fate had tossed together. He kissed the top of her head and took a breath. If the wedding orders her parents put in were any indications, the Galanis twins weren't allowed their own choices. But she could have them now. "What kinds of syrups, Breanna?"

"Your comment on filling the room isn't that far off. I love syrups, vanilla, mocha, chai, white chocolate, brown sugar cinnamon, seasonal favorites like pumpkin, peppermint, lavender."

"I know pumpkin and peppermint, but lavender?"

"More an add-in for tea. It's easiest to find in spring." She pulled back.

His arms ached to reach for her. To hold her again. To wipe away the hurt she hid too quickly in her eyes.

"Brown sugar cinnamon and chai are my favorites."

Then those would be here tomorrow. And a few others. He'd let the staff know to add a different new one each time a bottle was empty. That way she'd eventually have a nice stock without feeling like everything appeared all at once.

"All right. Was that so hard?"

"No." Breanna reached for the coffee mug.

"I have something for you." Sebastian had meant to wrap it, but the little box sitting on the cabinet would drive most of her days.

Breanna grinned. "A present?"

Yes. And no. "I thought this might come in handy." He pushed the box towards her.

"Handy. Interesting wording from a king." Breanna opened the box and nodded at the silver watch. It was delicate and well-made. But as her gaze roamed over it, he wished there'd been anything else in the box. A necklace or ring or… something.

Something that didn't scream *Sorry, but from now on the clock will rule your life. Time will be your enemy because there is never enough of it. Minutes will fly and hours evaporate.*

"Sebastian?" Breanna's hand was on his cheek.

"It's a nice gift. I suspect I will need a good time-piece to make sure I am where I need to be."

Sebastian nodded, then looked at it. "Yes." What else was there to say?

"Thank you." Breanna brushed her lips against his cheek, then put the watch on her wrist.

"So." She held up her arms as she spun in their kitchen. "What do you cook?"

There was no quick answer to that. He cooked a little of everything. Sebastian loved trying new recipes, creating his own. He was skilled enough now that most of the creations tasted good. That had not always been the case.

"Anything. I can make a mean scrambled egg." Sebastian winked. "Since traveling to Japan last year, I've started some days with *gohan* and an egg."

"So cooking is your hobby?"

"No. Cooking is just cooking." Sebastian headed to the fridge. "Do you eat eggs? These were never fertilized." One of his university professors had gotten very upset during a lecture about the different kinds of vegetarians. He didn't remember what started the man's forty-minute off-topic discussion, but he remembered the type the professor outlined.

He looked over his shoulder, and she was smiling. "If they were never fertilized, yes. No one has ever asked."

Another punch in the gut. No one had asked

his wife a basic question about her choices. He was used to that. As King, everyone assumed you got what you wanted. The reality was you got what others wanted for you.

Breanna hadn't worn a crown until yesterday. There was no reason for her not to be asked. Except for the Galanis family not caring what their daughters wanted.

"All right, well, I have rice in the steamer, and we can add the egg for protein. Then, time to get to know each other."

"Wonderful words to hear from your husband." She raised her coffee mug in a mock toast.

"So, you want to play twenty questions?" Breanna took a bite of the rice dish. It was savory and filling, but her stomach had no intention of settling. Get-to-know-you time was meant for dating. Meant for figuring out if you matched.

There was already a simple gold band on the ring finger of her left hand.

Sebastian's gaze was intense. The man's blue eyes seemed to say things that she suspected he had no intention of sharing.

"Let's think of it as more of a coffee date." Sebastian went to the machine and topped her mug off. Then he opened the sugar jar. "You tell me when."

He put one heaping spoon in. It looked just

like what she'd done. He'd paid attention. Why did that make her want to cry?

"That's good." Breanna's voice, broke but Sebastian didn't acknowledge it.

Her husband was kind. That was a good thing. A brilliant silver lining.

"Did you want to be queen?" Sebastian passed her the mug.

It nearly slipped through her fingers. There was a simple answer. Two little letters that changed nothing. What was the point of answering it now?

"That is not a coffee date question, Your Highness." She took a sip of her coffee, set it aside, then leaned her hands on the table. "Though to be honest, I've never been on a coffee date."

Or any date.

"Still, I think it's supposed to start with hobbies or favorite colors or what you were like growing up." Breanna playfully wagged a finger at him. "You like cooking. Do you enjoy baking too?"

Sebastian made a face.

"Was that grimace about me shifting the topic or about baking?" She leaned forward, enjoying the grin that appeared anytime she got close. Did he know he was doing that?

The king reached out and took her free hand, loosely playing with her fingers. A simple motion that shouldn't send heat racing through her.

"Maybe both."

"I had a roommate in college who loved to bake. She made cookies, cakes, the most beautiful pastries. Ask her to cook pasta and she'd throw up her hands. No interest. You'd think we were torturing her with such a suggestion!" She wrapped her ring finger around his, their matching gold bands glinting.

Small lines appeared around his eyes as he laughed, again. It filled the kitchen, and her stomach let go of some of the tension that seemed to be her constant companion.

"I feel that way about baking. It really is more science than anything else. No thank you."

"So, you didn't make the lemon cake for our wedding reception?" Breanna laid a hand over her chest, mock surprise making him laugh harder. It was a nice sight. The king in public was so controlled. So dutiful.

In his own kitchen though, he could laugh. When they were alone, she wanted this man.

"If I made it, it would have looked more like a lemon mush than cake."

"Lemon mush... I bet it still would have tasted lovely." Brenna didn't care so much about what the cake looked like. Until he'd kicked her parents out, their reception was a horror show. After?

Well, after they'd danced and danced. It was fun. Then the slow songs had started. She'd waited for him to take her hand for the first one, then made a quick escape when it seemed he didn't want to.

The second song, and the third and fourth, she'd spent in his arms, a feeling of safety seeping through her. Clearly the long day had scrambled some of her senses.

"Your Highness?" Raul walked into the kitchen and stopped. "Sorry, Your Highnesses." He nodded to Breanna.

Your Highness. She doubted she'd ever get used to that.

"It's early for the look of concern, Raul." Breanna held up her coffee mug. "Want a cup of coffee before you spill whatever difficult thing is on the tip of your tongue?"

Raul and her husband both stared at her with open mouths. "Do you not normally get asked to join the king and queen for coffee, or are those looks for something else?"

"I know the schedule says get to know the queen. But we have a situation." Raul looked at King Sebastian.

The queen. Not Breanna. The queen. Anyone could have fit that description provided they had a dress and willingly signed a contract. She was just the one he'd picked—or the one he'd been forced to pick when she'd exchanged places with Annie.

Breanna blew out a breath, trying to focus on the comment from Raul.

"An emergency?" It wasn't. At least, not a real one. Raul was stressed but not bent in trauma. Sebastian, and now she, had duties as royals, but they also needed a life.

"Uh—"

"If you have to think on it, then it's not." It was day one of being queen. Maybe she shouldn't assert herself now, but if she didn't start right away, she might lose the gumption. Her husband needed a hobby and time to be Sebastian, not just the king.

And she refused to wear her crown, metaphorically or otherwise, before nine, unless it was absolutely necessary.

"So, coffee time. The king and I are not responding to business before nine a.m. or after eight p.m." She wasn't sure the times would stick, but whether they fluctuated or not, the idea was what mattered.

"Breanna," Sebastian's voice was soft, not quite a rebuke, but close enough.

Ignoring the twinge in her stomach, she went to the small mug stand and grabbed one for Raul. "We don't have syrups." She made a playful face at Sebastian, but he didn't react.

The king stood before her now. The duty-bound man who gave her a wristwatch the day after marrying her.

"So, cream and sugar or black?" Her voice wobbled, but she kept the smile on her face.

Raul looked to Sebastian, but the king didn't say anything. "Um…black, Your Highness."

"Breanna. Call me Breanna." She passed him the cup.

"We have a duty, Breanna." Sebastian was ramrod straight. The man who'd played with her fingers and kissed her head when she was panicking this morning was lost. But he was there, she'd seen him. He just had let go a little.

"We also have lives." She held up her hand before Sebastian could say anything else. Maybe she hadn't wanted this life. But she was making the best of it. Period.

"Raul, tell me about yourself." Color drained from the man's face, and she sighed. "All right, take a deep breath. We will start the actual work in an hour. Until then, we were talking hobbies. Sebastian claims he doesn't have any, but we both know it's cooking, right?"

This time Raul didn't look to the king. Instead, he laughed, and she saw Sebastian take a deep breath. Her husband was not used to putting off work.

Even the day after their wedding. She tried not to let that sting. This was a marriage of convenience. In the twenty-first century, it looked a little different, but that didn't change the truth. Her husband didn't want her.

He'd wanted a bride, and a queen. The person

standing there didn't really matter. As exchangeable as pieces of paper placed in a hat.

But she needed to have some boundaries. Something to ground her.

"Yes. And I assume based on the sewing equipment the team brought to your room, you like creating new things."

It was more than that. She liked finding and repurposing old things. Rehabbing clothes that others thought were too outdated or damaged. Almost one hundred billion garments were made a year, and nearly ninety percent of materials ended up in landfills. Less than one percent was rehabbed or recycled, but she was trying to do her part.

It was a stance her parents refused to understand. Yes, her closet could contain a new outfit every day. A couture item designed just for her never to be worn again. Her family's budget wouldn't even notice a dent.

But what was the purpose of that?

"Breanna, we really need to discuss the situation." Sebastian motioned for Raul to continue.

This time Raul didn't look to her for confirmation. Instead, he reached for the tablet next to him and started reciting off the "issues."

None of which sounded like they were more than the average headache. A frustration, but hardly something that had to be started right away.

In the passing moments, it had become clear

that she wasn't needed. She looked at her new watch, then slid off the stool. She waited to see if her husband would say anything, then hoped to hear his voice as she walked to the door.

He never raised his head from the tablet.

A day after her wedding and already an afterthought…

CHAPTER FIVE

"WHAT DO YOU THINK, Breanna?" Sebastian lifted his head from the tablet and was shocked to find her gone. "Breanna?"

Color crept up Raul's neck. "She left."

"Left?" Sebastian shook his head and tried to remember if she'd said goodbye.

"About twenty minutes ago, Your Highness."

Twenty minutes.

He pushed his hands through his hair and looked at her coffee mug sitting in front of the stool where she'd sat joking with him about hobbies and setting a schedule. How could he have missed that?

Except he knew how. When he focused on duty, he drowned everything else out. It was a trick he'd learned as a child, that way his focus never drifted to things he'd rather do. Instead, his mind stayed in the present. Laser-focused on the responsibilities given him though a roll of the universal dice of fate.

It worked well when he was a child. Even as

an adult—but as a husband it left more than a little to be desired.

"I think we are done for now. Reach out to Alessio. The art nonprofits usually like having him at their events. I agree that more notice would have been nice, but everyone gets busy, and things fall through the cracks. I am not surprised the requests for royal attendance came late."

Raul made a few notes. "If Prince Alessio and Princess Brie are unable to attend?"

"Then I will figure out how to be in three places at once." He and Breanna were already scheduled to make appearances at two other locations that day. A ribbon cutting and a speech given by a local celebrity on a topic he couldn't quite remember.

Breanna liked fiber arts. That was something she could highlight as the queen. Show off her pieces and work. Encourage others. Between her and Alessio, the royal family was quite artistic.

Sebastian pushed himself away from the counter. He needed to find Breanna. This was supposed to be their day together. Time to get to know each other.

And he'd let duty get in the way. It was necessary, but he could have explained better.

He quickly rinsed the mug, hung it back in its place, then went to find his bride. She'd be in her rooms. Mostly because he hadn't taken her on a tour of the palace yet.

There were many excuses he could give for that, but none of them mattered.

He raised his hand, knocked on her suite door. Her voice gave him entry, and he opened the door.

Breanna was bent over her large workbench. The ugliest dress he'd ever seen lay on top of it. He stood there waiting for her angry snap. He'd earned this one. Whatever she wanted to let out, he'd take it.

But the silence carried on, and his wife's eyes never left her project.

Finally, she grabbed some tool, and then started doing something to the garment on her bench. The sleeves fell away, but it didn't improve the garment's look all that much. "Did you need something, Sebastian?"

"It's all right if you want to yell at me." Maybe she wanted permission? His father often gave it to his mother when they had a spat. Sebastian didn't remember her ever raising her voice, but the option was there.

An option Samantha had never needed. When she'd felt like lashing out, she had not held back. She'd told him all the things she'd change when she was queen. How he'd not recognized that was all she wanted was beyond him now. *Love blinded you.*

The tool clattered to the table. "Why would I yell at you?" Breanna's dark eyes looked genuinely shocked.

"I ignored you." Heat stole along his collar. Married less than a day and he'd ignored the woman in front of him when they were supposed to be getting to know each other. Duty came first, but he should have noticed her leaving.

"An apology would be nice. But why yell? I know what this marriage is. What I am." There was no malice in the words. No emotion at all.

Just an acceptance that nearly sent him to his knees. Funny, he'd always thought anger was the worst emotion. But her quiet statement hurt more than any angry words Samantha had thrown at him.

"Breanna, I am so sorry. I got caught up in the emergency."

"No." She leaned against the table and crossed her arms. "I appreciate the apology, but that was not an emergency."

He didn't want to squabble, but he needed her to understand their roles.

"What might not look like an emergency to those not wearing crowns has to be treated as an emergency by those who are."

One of his father's favorite refrains.

"I know a gala event might not seem like an emergency."

"No." Breanna shook her head. "A gala event is *not* an emergency."

He smiled, but he knew the motion was tight. "It is to the nonprofit."

"No." Breanna laughed. "It is not."

"Everyone is struggling."

"No, they *are not*." Breanna pushed away from the table. "Princess Brie's tourism board has brought back all the tourists we lost during the recession, plus others who've never visited. Yes, there are those still struggling, but it is not the same situation the country was in a year ago. And *no one* throwing a gala is in danger."

"The nonprofit—"

Her hand pressed against his chest. "Would not be spending hard-earned coin on an expensive gala when they are in danger. That is something you do when you have money to spare and are looking for bigger donors. It is a *good* sign."

Her words struck him. He knew what was required of him as a prince, and a king, but Sebastian's life was as far from normal as possible. Attendance at events. Hosting diplomats. Staying politically neutral. It was a delicate balancing act.

But his day-to-day looked nothing like that of the people of Celiana.

"The last few years—"

"Were rough." Breanna ran her finger along his chin. "But that changed when your brother married Brie. The choice to have a small wedding for us was a good one." She swallowed, looking away for a moment.

He couldn't blame her. Brie and Alessio's wedding had been a giant party. Even though they'd made sure the cost was far from the weddings most expected of the crown. It could have been had in the smallest room on the island, with no music, and the happiness from his brother and sister-in-law would have carried the event.

The same couldn't be said for the affair they had. Even though he'd enjoyed dancing with Breanna most of the evening. There was no love in the air. No music created by two souls who never wished to be parted.

"People are still focused on replenishing savings, but they are not struggling like they were. So, it was a good idea." Whether his wife was trying to convince herself by repeating the idea or convince him didn't really matter.

Rationally, he knew that made sense. And he'd seen the metrics from the tourism industry, and others. It was good. But it wasn't the full story of the crown.

A life of service. Always. That was what the king and queen of Celiana owed the country.

"That doesn't change the fact that we need to be at events." It was their role. Draw attention to projects needing it—the power of influence.

"Which events do we pass along our regrets to?" Breanna raised her chin, her eyes brimming with challenge as she crossed her arms. He wanted her to touch him again, to comfort him.

"We don't." He hated the stress he saw fly through her eyes. But influence was a fickle beast. A cup overflowing could dry up with the wrong words or missed opportunity. He wore the crown, but the influence his father had cultivated, the embers his brother had kept warm when he'd floundered…it could disappear.

Sebastian didn't care about the influence for himself, but the nonprofits, the tourists, the people gained something from it. He would not strip that from them for his own selfish desires.

Breanna laughed, though the bell-like sound held no humor. "Seriously, Sebastian, you do get to have time off. You are just a man, after all."

"The crown does not rest."

Dear God, it was like his father's soul had just overtaken him.

The man's presence even a few years after his passing was still felt everywhere.

"That is nonsense."

Breanna wasn't used to a life of duty. The Galanis family had more money than nearly everyone on the island. Her family did not care what their influence brought for others. He doubted Lucas Galanis was capable of thinking of anything besides his own bank account.

Breanna and her sister had wanted for nothing. *Except affection.*

His life had been similarly privileged, similarly lacking in affection from his father and to some extent his mother. But it was duty, not coin, that drove his father's ambitions. The deep knowledge ingrained in each royal that they worked for the people of Celiana.

He'd had one vacation. A few days skiing before his tenth birthday. A last hurrah before the real work of his life started. Was that unfair? Sure. But fairness was not what this world was built on.

During the year where he'd rebelled, he'd still attended the events required of him. Alessio had had to pick up most of the day duties, and he'd figured out a way to get the country out of the economic depression with his bride lotto. However, he'd arrived when he'd absolutely had to. Even the night when he and Samantha had broken up, he'd gone to the state dinner. Broken. Bitter. And late. But still in attendance.

"It can be fun. As queen, you can focus on specific charitable events." He pointed to the dress. "There are many arts functions that would love to display any of the garment talents you have."

Breanna shook her head. "No. This—" she gestured to the dress "—is just for me. Mine. Something no one can take from me."

He wasn't trying to take it. Just expand it. Use her knowledge and expertise to help others. She was queen now. She'd met him at the altar. Chosen this path. "You're the queen now. Nothing is just for you, anymore."

"We shall see about that."

He didn't argue. She'd come to understand the

truth soon enough. "Would you like a tour of the palace?"

She closed her eyes for a moment, then turned a brilliant smile to him. "I suppose it is a good idea to know my away around my home."

"Home." He chuckled. "I don't think I've ever referred to the palace as home. It's not really mine, after all."

Once more the truth slipped out. He was typically very good at keeping his personal truths locked away. Sometimes he pushed them far enough away he almost forgot they were there.

Almost.

Breanna didn't push back though. Instead, she put her tools away, then looked at him. "Ready when you are."

CHAPTER SIX

THE TINY CROWN on her head didn't weigh much. Rationally she knew that. But it still felt like it was digging into her scalp as she greeted yet another guest at the fundraising event that she was more certain than ever was not an emergency.

"You are doing well." Sebastian's words were soft as he leaned over and pushed a hair that had fallen from the elaborate updo from her face. His fingers brushed her cheek, lingering for just a moment before turning back to the guests.

Well. A word her father had used to make sure she and Annie knew they could do better. Four letters that fell far short of best. And if you weren't the best, why bother?

Sebastian meant it that way, too. Not in the cruel manner, but in the "helpful" you-will-get-there way. The supportive king instructing his brand-new queen. There was no anger. No upset.

Because he'd expected his pick to struggle with the adjustment at first. This wasn't an issue with Breanna. It was an issue with "the queen."

An interchangeable bride the crown would sculpt. Anyone could be standing here and Sebastian would support them.

"You look tired." The woman's kind words were sweet as she squeezed Breanna's hand.

"I'm fine. But thank you."

The woman moved to Sebastian. Her statement not one of a real concern, but a passing phrase. But it meant others could see her forced smile.

But how could she offer more? Her toes ached and her head pounded. She'd been on her feet for almost fifteen hours straight. Exhaustion had stopped nipping at her heels hours ago.

Now it was the pure force of pride keeping her upright. She was not going to collapse in public. With any luck, their commitment was over as soon as the receiving line ended. After all, the event had ended almost an hour ago.

Raul came up and offered Sebastian, and then her, water. "The receiving line just closed at the other end. It should be done in about an hour."

Breanna couldn't stop the harsh laugh escaping her lips. An hour. *An hour.* Sebastian stepped closer and put an arm around her. She leaned into him. Needing to give her feet some relief from the torture devices on her toes.

"It will be all right." His words were kind, but they did little to help her in the moment.

How did he manage this? They'd been on the go every moment since their wedding. She was maintaining some boundaries. Refusing to start her day before a certain hour might not seem like much, but in the palace, it was rebellion.

She wasn't sure Sebastian had any boundaries at all. The man said yes to everything.

"Take a deep breath." He shook the next person's hand. His arm on her waist tugged just slightly. He was offering to pull her close. Giving her some of his strength. Not pressuring, but the unspoken offer was clear.

She took it. Desperate times called for desperate measures. And standing close to her husband, enjoying the scent of him, the comfort he offered, was as far from desperate as possible. "I need different shoes."

Sebastian looked at her feet, then motioned with his free hand back to Raul. "Find the queen some flats."

"Oh." Raul was off before Breanna managed any other words. She'd meant the statement as a reminder to herself to wear flats for the next event. Like she'd have a choice. Her toes might rebel if she tried to put them in heels tomorrow.

She'd watched her husband swallow a yawn as he reached for the next guest's hand. The man was skilled at hiding exhaustion, but if you looked for it, it wasn't hard to see. He gave the country everything—he needed something for himself.

"The queen is stepping into her role quite

nicely." Sebastian nodded to the gentleman, then turned to greet the next guest.

The queen. Not Breanna. Here she was the title. Nothing more. Anyone with the crown and the title could be here, and the line would form.

When the end of the line came into view, Breanna bounced, then winced. Wherever Raul had gone for flats, it was a futile effort now.

She started to lean her head against Sebastian's shoulder, then snapped it back up. Getting support from him was nice. And she needed it. That did not mean she needed to rest her head on his shoulder.

"Almost done." He squeezed her as the final two people came into view. "We helped raise a lot of money tonight. You've done wonderfully."

They'd done well. But money would have come in without them. Maybe not quite as much. People had purchased tickets to the fundraiser long before the king and queen's attendance was announced. So, the nonprofit would have made a hefty profit.

Then Sebastian had offered a reception line as a fundraiser. Now the pot was overflowing. Literally. A nice perk for a group that wouldn't have to fundraise much for the next year but hardly an emergency. If everything was an emergency, then nothing was.

Her husband needed some boundaries. If only for her own sanity.

Sebastian gave their goodbyes to the organizers as she smiled. The neurons not focused on the pain radiating down her feet were an exhausted mush too far gone to say much more than have a nice night. They waved and started towards the car.

She took two steps, then let out a sigh. "Hold up." She put a hand on her husband's shoulder and slipped one heel, then the other, off her feet.

The cold tile was heaven. "Ooh." Her toes rejoiced as they were finally allowed a little more freedom. Her hose refused to give them a full range of motion, but she'd take what she could get.

Breanna resolved to donate these torture heels. Those monstrosities were never going back on her feet. Never!

"We aren't at the car yet." Sebastian looked at her bare feet, then into the distance she had no plans on crossing in the heels.

"I know." She patted his arm, then started towards the car. "But I refuse to hobble my way there. I can't stand the way those things—" she glared at the offending shoes "—find every possible way to make my feet scream!"

"You'll tear your hose."

"Congratulations, Your Highness." Breanna giggled, exhaustion making her a little punchy. "I think you found the argument least likely to move me."

If she had her way, the hose in her top drawer would vanish. Flimsy material that was confining was the work of black magic—you would not convince her otherwise. Yet the dowager queen never set foot outside the palace without nude hose covering her legs.

It was expected of queens. For reasons no one could explain to her because hose weren't even technically invented until 1959. A fact she had not known until she was adding it to her arsenal of reasons why she had no intention of keeping up that tradition.

"The car isn't far." Sebastian took a breath. "What if you hurt your feet?"

She looked at him, really looked at him for the first time this evening. The lines under his eyes were darker, and worry lines were etched along his lips. Without thinking, she raised her free hand and ran her thumb along his chin.

His sigh echoed in the empty room, and his head leaned against her hand, like she was pulling a little of the exhaustion from his tired frame.

She took a breath and softened her tone. "I appreciate the concern. I do. But these heels will hurt my feet more than the pristine floors. And sometimes it is fun to be spontaneous. Take your shoes off, Your Highness."

Sebastian chuckled but shook his head. "A king is supposed to keep his shoes on."

"Says who?" Breanna stuck her bare feet out

from under the full-length gown she had on. "Your queen is almost barefoot."

"She is." He stepped towards her, and the air in the room vanished as he smiled at her. He was close. So close.

"My queen is very cute almost barefoot." Huskiness coated his tone as he closed the bit of distance between them.

Was he going to kiss her? There was a glint in his eyes. A mischievousness.

She wanted him to. "Come on, Your Highness?" Was she daring him to take off his shoes? Or kiss her.

"Breanna." Sebastian paused then scooped her up.

"Ooh!" She instantly wrapped her arms around his shoulders. The relief in her digits sent a groan through her as she flexed her feet. He hadn't kissed her. That was fine. Picking her up was sweet. It was.

The tiny burst of disappointment was just from exhaustion.

"See." His lips were so close to hers. "You needed—" he pulled back, a yawn escaping his mouth "—the relief."

"Yes." She kissed his cheek. For a moment she could pretend this was a date. Or a fun night out. That they were just two people having a good time. Caring for each other.

Not a husband and wife…a king and queen… who barely knew each other.

"But you are exhausted, too. Who takes care of you?"

"I am the king." Sebastian nodded to the man opening the door and waited a moment as the other doorman rushed to the waiting car to open that door.

He slid her into her seat, and the relief in her aching back nearly brought tears to her eyes.

Sebastian climbed in next to her and told the driver they were ready. It would be easy to close her eyes and drift into sleep until they were at the palace. But she had so little alone time with the man she called husband.

"Who takes care of you?" Breanna pushed again.

"I told you." Sebastian closed his eyes and leaned his head back. It was like the final charge of his internal battery was gone.

"No." Breanna shook her head. "I am king."

His eyes popped open and he chuckled, his hand reaching for hers. "That sounds nothing like me."

"The words are an exact replica." Breanna squeezed his hand. "Who takes care of you?"

Sebastian pulled her hand to his lips, quickly brushing them across her knuckles. Her breath caught.

"I am the king." He let out a sigh so heavy it

sounded like it carried the weight of the country. "No one needs to take care of me."

He closed his eyes again.

All her words were trapped in her throat. What was she supposed to say to such nonsense?

"Everyone needs care."

The only response she got was soft snores, but his hand still cradled hers.

CHAPTER SEVEN

BREANNA REACHED FOR her toes, groaning as the muscles in her lower back cried out. She was active. She'd biked nearly every day and lifted light weights. The only trouble she had was heavy menstrual cycles, which were now well-controlled with an IUD. She was at peak physical condition according to her doctor at the appointment she'd had a month before Sebastian arrived at her door.

And the crown had worn her into the ground in weeks. Her feet had more blisters than toes, and no matter the amount of stretches she did in the morning and before bed, her body ached when she woke. How did Sebastian maintain this life?

He doesn't.

The thought pierced her mind as she looked over the schedule her assistant always forwarded just after midnight. A full day—like every day.

And like most days, she wasn't seeing her husband until a dinner engagement they were attending with Prince Alessio and Princess Brie. The man was gone before she woke.

Off to some meeting. Attending some function. Working on a task that didn't really need doing. How many things could a king really be expected to do before eight? Apparently far too many.

"Breanna?" That was her husband's voice. But according to his schedule, he was supposed to be handling personal correspondences this morning. A mountain of letters arrived with each post. He'd respond to so many that tonight he'd stretch his fingers when he thought no one looking. Bending them, flexing and balling them into a fist. Hurting but saying nothing.

She turned to look at the door to her work room. "Yes?"

Her husband stepped into her room, and she smiled. He was here. To spend some time with her. Since the morning after their wedding, they'd really only seen each other at events. In the car and in a few passing moments in the hall.

He was kind, asking after her needs. He'd never gotten close enough to make her think he was going to kiss her though. That night at the fundraiser was a one-off moment. Maybe she'd been so tired, her memory was playing tricks on her.

Her husband checked in on her. Far more than her parents had ever managed.

Part of her almost wished he didn't bother. If King Sebastian refused to acknowledge her, if it was clear that she was just a thing he needed to support his throne, to stop the constant wave of people harassing women even loosely attached to him, then she could adjust. Accept the life she had to protect Annie.

After all…filling a role was something she'd always done. Quiet daughter. Respectful daughter. Exchangeable daughter. If only the location had shifted, from the compound to the palace, she'd adjust easily.

But he cared for her when she was tired. Kicked her parents out of their wedding reception when it was clear that they were cruel. Got her coffee syrups and made veggie dishes that were clearly marked in the fridge—when—she had no idea.

It was the grounds for so much more than they had.

He was overburdened. If she found a way to give him peace, found a way to have him accept the need for boundaries, they had a chance to not spend the rest of their lives as strangers.

To give themselves a chance at more. Surely that chance was something they should reach for.

"Sebastian. Are you here to join me for coffee? I got my cup from our kitchen a few minutes ago. I can ring—" The words died on her lip as a woman who couldn't have been more than five feet tall stepped from behind him. Around her neck hung a measuring tape, and she had a box filled with tools Breanna didn't recognize.

"Where can I set this, Your Highness? It's heavy." Her thick accent accentuated each word.

"Of course." Breanna moved quickly folding her project but careful to make sure the pins holding the material in place stayed where they were meant to be. "You should have asked the king to carry your things."

She winked at her husband and immediately hated the joke as his shoulders stiffened.

"I offered Olga more than one chance to let me handle the box. She's as stubborn as my wife."

"Then we shall get along fine." Breanna clapped her hands, hoping this jest would remove some of the tension in his body.

Olga hmphed as she set the box down and then looked at the queen. The woman's eyes were sharp, but the assessment held no malice. After the weeks she'd had in the palace, it was refreshing.

"You are tallish."

Ish? Breanna wasn't sure what to make of that. She was a little over five foot seven. Average height. Though to a woman who had to look up at the world, she supposed most people qualified as tallish.

"Good feet." She pointed, then started pulling things from her box.

"They don't feel so good." Breanna glared at the sores on her toes, then made a silly face at her husband.

"Because your shoes don't fit." Sebastian stepped beside her. Not quite touching but close enough that if she moved even a little, they'd brush sides.

Except he didn't get any closer. It was silly to be upset by that. But the flicker she'd felt at the fundraiser had been snuffed out.

If it was ever there to begin with.

"They fit before I stood in them for hours on hours on hours on hours."

Her husband held up his hands. "I get it. I should have put a cap on the receiving line."

That was more than she'd expected him to acknowledge. "Yes. You should have." She bumped his hip with hers. Why did she want to touch him?

Sebastian wrapped his arm around her waist, just like he'd done the night they'd met, and that night in the receiving line. But unlike those times, he pulled away quickly. Like she'd burned him. Or more likely, because he didn't want to touch her.

Her chest burned as she sucked in a breath. Trying to focus on the task at hand.

"So I am here to fit you for shoes. Perfect ones. Ones that will not do that." Olga tsked as she pointed to the sores on Breanna's feet.

"They wouldn't if I wasn't standing so long."

"But you are queen." Olga said the words, but it was Sebastian's nod that tore through her.

This was the expectation. This was what she was supposed to do. She was supposed to stand all the time. Supposed to put everyone's needs before her own.

She'd done that her whole life. Breanna was good at it. But there'd been downtime, too. Time for herself. Filled with thread and bobbles, and laughter and rest.

Celiana was important. The royal family was important, but they were more than their positions. Weren't they?

Sebastian was more than the title. More than the king. The crown didn't have to be the only thing people saw.

"So, I need shoes that will let me stand for hours every day." She pointed to Olga's box. "What magic is in there to allow such a thing?"

Olga pulled a few things out and started gesturing for her to sit. A woman of few words, but the demands were clear.

"I need to see to my correspondence."

"Oh. I thought you'd stay?" If only there were a way to bite back that request. She'd hoped he'd adjusted his schedule. More than just to drop a shoemaker at her door and wish her good morning.

"Behind schedule. I'm going to have to skip lunch to get it all written up." He lifted a hand and headed for the door.

"Sebas—" But her husband was already gone.

She followed Olga's demands while plotting out her next move. One thing was certain. Sebastian was not skipping lunch.

Sebastian shook his hand, then rolled his wrists, even though he knew it wouldn't stop the pins-and-needles feeling trickling from his elbow to the tips of his fingers.

His schedule was off today, but the trip to see Breanna was worth it. The image of his wife popped into his head. He'd wanted to kiss her the night of the fundraiser. Wanted to pull her close, hold her and never let go.

But he'd promised her separate lives. A king and queen in title. Lives of their own. He couldn't ask for a change when she was a newly minted queen. She was overwhelmed. Finding her place.

He would not take advantage of that.

Sebastian stifled a yawn. No one was here to see the exhaustion, but the habit was ingrained in him. Only Breanna had seen him yawn in years.

"Kings do not get tired. They are perfection for their people."

Words his father had said during their early-morning walks, back when he'd still complained about the exhaustion that was his constant companion.

He read the letter over, for the third time. Nothing seemed to stick this morning.

The door to the office opened, but he didn't look up. If he allowed himself to get distracted now, then he'd never get through all of this. Sebastian's schedule was already pushed to the extremes today.

"Sebastian?"

"Hello, Breanna. Did Olga finish your shoes?" He tried to read the letter in front of him and figure out a quick way to sign a response.

If only the letters on the page stayed still.

"Sebastian, I can hear your stomach gurgling from here." She stepped to the desk and took the letter from his hands. She looked at it, then leaned over him, taking the pen from his other hand.

Breanna's scent infiltrated his nose. His body tightened, then softened, like a strong breeze that suddenly shifts. He took a deep breath, letting himself settle. She was here. His wife.

"Now sign your name." Breanna pushed the pen back in his hand.

He blinked, then looked at the short note she'd written on the paper the staff had left for this letter's response.

Happy birthday, Serena. Sixteen is a wonderful time. We hope that your days are blessed with adventure and growth. Enjoy!

A birthday letter. A note that should have been so easy to push out. Yet he'd read the words multiple times without his mind clicking. Shame there wasn't time for a nap.

He quickly signed his name above Breanna's.

"Serena won't know it, but this is the first letter signed by the queen."

"Uh-huh." Breanna grabbed the rest of the correspondence.

"Wait. What are…" Sebastian stood as she started towards the office door. There were at least a dozen left to go. Probably more.

Breanna opened the door. "Come on. He needs to eat." She sighed then looked over her shoulder. "Raul wants you to know that I am forcing this issue and that he had nothing to do with it." She looked back through the door. "Does that cover it?"

It must have, because Raul marched in with a tray of food, set it on the table by the unlit fireplace, and vanished.

"You need to eat." Breanna grabbed his hand and pulled him towards the table.

"I *need* to—"

Her finger lay over his lips. "You need to eat. So that is what we are going to do, Your Highness."

"Your Highness…? Guess you're cross with me." Sebastian sat at the table, happy when she sat on the other side.

Breanna lifted the lid of the plate. "Not cross. Worried."

He opened his mouth, and she held up the finger that had pressed against his lips moments ago. "If you are about to do anything other than eat the veggies, hummus and egg salad, you can do it after."

She dipped a veggie in hummus took a bite, then motioned for him to do the same.

Tightness hovered in his throat. He was the king. No one looked after him. No one.

"Thank you."

"You are welcome. Now, eat." She pointed to his dish. "You look like hell."

"Only Alessio ever tells me that."

"Well, I am your queen, so..." Breanna huffed as she drove her fork into the salad.

They ate in a comfortable silence as he wolfed down the lunch she'd had prepared and let out a soft sigh. He felt better. "Thank you."

"You are welcome." Breanna smiled, then pointed to the desk. "How about I sort while you sign."

"Teamwork?" Sebastian started to reach for her hand, but stopped himself. "Umm, I don't want to hold you up. You don't have to help."

"I am offering. There is a difference." She looked at his hand, the one that had not reached for hers, then stood and grabbed the pile, sifting through the letters quickly.

He followed, very aware of his bride's presence at his side as she handed him one letter at a time.

"Birthday."

"Anniversary."

"Graduating with a master's degree in bio-chemistry. Wow."

He signed each one with a quick note, and the pile was nearly gone before he realized it.

"Wow." Breanna read the last one.

"Another graduation?"

Sebastian started to reach for it, but she shook her head. A look he couldn't quite interpret coming over her eyes.

"No. Anniversary. Fifty years. Fifty years. Their daughter requested the note. She gushes over how her parents are soulmates. How lucky she is to watch their love." She let out a breath. "Must be something special."

Something we don't have.

She didn't say the words but passed him the note.

He wrote a quick congratulations, aware of the shift in the room.

"Do you believe in soulmates?" The question was out, and he wished there was a way to pop it back in. That was a question to ask on a date. Or with a friend. It was not a question to lay at his wife's feet.

A wife he'd known for weeks. A wife he'd married days after a public announcement. A wife he rarely saw.

"No." There was no hesitation. "I am glad that others believe, but no. I do not feel like there is one perfect person in the world for me. Relationships take work. Good ones involve friendship and respect."

There was no way to ignore the pinch in his stomach that she didn't mention love or caring in her thoughts on marriage. Why should she? It wasn't what their marriage was built on. No, they didn't even have friendship. Though the respect was there. At least on his side.

Breanna sat on the desk, now clear of the notes he'd thought would take twice as long. "You have thirty minutes until your next appointment." She grinned as she tapped the watch on her wrist. The gift he'd given her the day after their wedding.

It was a nice watch, but he couldn't help but wish that he'd given her something more Breanna. Something that said he knew her.

Except outside of liking to sew and wanting to sleep in until seven, he knew very little about his wife.

"So what shall we do with the extra thirty minutes?" Breanna raised her brow as though she was asking something truly scandalous. "We could think of it as playing hooky."

"We could." He leaned closer. "The king and his queen."

"Or Sebastian and Breanna. There is no one here right now. No crowns." She patted her head, then patted his. "Nope. No crown."

"Had to check?" He laughed and put his hands on her hips. Heat, need and things he shouldn't want raced through him.

"It does seem like one might live on your head all the time."

"Very funny, *Your Highness*." He laughed, pulling her into his lap. His touch was light. If she wanted to move, she could. This wasn't in the script of their separate lives' union. But then, neither was her showing up with lunch and making him eat.

What if they could have more?

Breanna poked his forehead. "You are lost in thought. Want me to move?"

"No." His arms wrapped around her.

Kiss her. Kiss her.

The mantra repeated in brain, screaming at him to take the next step.

Then phone on the desk buzzed, and he could tell by the instant fall of her face that she knew something else was popping in. He could ignore it. He could.

Except…this was the life of a king and queen. The call of duty for one who knew nothing else. If he failed in his duty, others got hurt.

This was his life. All he was.

Sebastian took a deep breath, pushed on the

speaker, and heard Raul's out-of-breath sigh. "Any chance you can do a short video call with the director of Leaps for Launch?"

"Leaps for Launch?" Breanna asked as she slid off his lap. Whatever moment they'd been about to have was gone.

"A new nonprofit." Raul answered for him through the phone. "They are trying to set up micro loans for small businesses. A real leg up, but the idea is having some trouble gaining ground. Royal backing is good, but a business-person would be better."

"Right now, all we have is royal backing." Sebastian reached for the pen he'd used to sign his name to dozens of letters. Now it was note-taking time.

"Not like royal backing is nothing." Breanna moved around the desk, resignation clear on her features.

"Raul." Sebastian looked at Breanna, smiled, then continued. "Give me five minutes to check in with my wife, then patch the call through."

He hung up the phone. "Thank you for your help with the letters and for lunch."

"Of course." Breanna crossed her arms, then uncrossed them, then crossed them again. The easiness they'd had before Raul's call vanished.

"If you need a businessperson, why not ask Brie to reach out to her brother? He's broken with their parents now. Beau might be willing to provide some backing."

"His break with the Ailiono is fairly recent. He and Brie haven't had much of a chance to get to know each other in their new relationship. He might not be up to it." But if he stepped in as a backer, it would send a powerful message to the island.

But would he?

Sebastian hadn't interacted with Beau Ailiono much. Beau was as much his father's protégé as Sebastian was his father's. Neither side was discussing the cause of the break, but given what Brie had experienced, he was inclined to side with Beau.

"The answer to every unasked question is no." Breanna shrugged. "What if I reach out to Brie and see what she thinks?"

A wave of appreciation washed through him. He didn't need to add anything to the mental list that seemed to run miles long through his soul. A to-do list that the king had no power to ever finish. All the checkmarks only vanished when another took his throne.

"That would be very helpful." Sebastian nodded. "Thank you." He looked at his watch. "We still have two minutes."

"Right." Breanna balled her fists and then looked over her shoulder at the door, "I will gift those to you, Your Highness. Spend them well."

The ache in his stomach now had nothing to do with hunger. He wanted to go after her. Ask her to stay with him for the day, chat, do fun things. Things that weren't on his schedule.

The phone rang, and reality slipped in. Duty called...literally.

CHAPTER EIGHT

"YOU LOOK LIKE HELL. I know no one else will say that. But it is still true." Alessio's muttered words were soft enough not to draw attention to them from other bystanders, but the bite was still strong.

"My wife said that exact thing this morning." Sebastian chuckled as his gaze found Breanna. She was dressed in a floor-length red beaded gown. One shoulder was bare while the other had a cap sleeve. It was elegant, queen-like. With a slit up the side that made his mouth water every time his eyes landed on her.

Alessio lifted his champagne flute in her general direction. "Then to our new queen."

Sebastian followed the motion. "To the new... queen." The word *queen* was heavy on his tongue. Breanna was more than that. So much more.

At least until he put the crown on her head.

"But you still look like hell." His brother blew out a breath. "You need to rest more."

"Said so simply." Sebastian tipped his head to

one of the guests as they made eye contact. To-night was more about the politicians and their goals for Celiana, but the royal family's attendance was still expected.

Expected. One of his father's favorites. Such a foul word. One that drove everything about his life. About Breanna's life.

He hated the word, but also knew that if he didn't play this role, then someone else would have to.

Someone else had.

The man beside him now. The man that it would fall to again if he failed.

"The crown—"

"Is heavy." Sebastian slapped his brother's shoulder as their wives walked up. He had no intention of continuing a conversation for which there was no resolution.

Brie slipped into Alessio's arms; he squeezed her tightly. While Breanna stepped close to him. A respectful distance between the two.

This afternoon she'd been on his lap. Laughing and joking. And looking oh, so kissable. For a moment it felt like the contract they had wasn't needed. Like maybe…

And he'd taken that phone call. Had to take a phone call.

He couldn't stop the sigh echoing from his lips. It would be so easy to want what Alessio and Brie had. To reach for Breanna and hope his queen wanted the same. But duty demanded he put the kingdom first. No one should settle for being second to that.

"Brie is going to reach out to Beau about Leaps for Launch." Breanna whispered as she waved to a guest who was walking their way.

"Do you know him?" Sebastian asked. The gentleman was a giant. A damn handsome giant. A well-known playboy strolling towards Breanna.

And his wife looked happier than he'd ever seen her.

"Yes. That is Hector Stevio. I thought everyone on the island knew Hector." She pushed on Sebastian's arm.

Knew of him was probably a better statement. And she was practically bouncing.

"Look at you!" Hector stepped up and bowed to the queen, then turned his attention to the other royals, bowing to them.

"I think you are supposed to bow to the king first." Breanna laughed and then offered her hand to Hector.

Sebastian took a deep breath as he watched his wife visibly relax. It was hard not to wish that she smiled at him like that.

"I guess you shall have to school me in royal protocol, Your Highness." Hector winked at the queen, then dipped his head to Sebastian. "Your Highness."

Sebastian nodded, his eyes glued to the play-boy who'd dated most of the island's leading men and women. Hector was famous, or infamous, depending on the storyteller, for his parties, his businesses, his life. The man could turn a piece of straw into gold. Then the business got boring for him—at least that was the story—and he sold it.

Started the game over. Never satisfied.

And now he was looking at Breanna as though she was the top prize in the room. Which she was.

"The dance floor is empty, my queen. Can I have this dance?" Hector offered his hand to Bre-anna.

His wife placed her hand in the playboy's hand and walked with him to the dance floor. Hec-tor pulled her close, and the air evaporated from the room. Breanna was glowing. She was happy. There was no hint of hesitation.

Something the weeks in the palace hadn't granted her. Something he didn't expect to ever be able to fully give her. She had a crown, a title and duty.

Just like him.

"Breathe, brother." Alessio passed the cham-pagne flute to one of the waitstaff. Then took Sebastian's and passed it over too, waving away the offer of more for both of them.

"They are childhood friends." Brie leaned around her husband, her brow raising exactly as his wife's did. "She is trying to get his help with the Leaps for Launch, too. But given his reputation for spinning something up and then selling it, she thinks Beau might be a better spokesman."

"That's nice." Alessio's grin was clearly meant more for Brie than him. "Isn't it, brother?"

"Yes. Nice." Sebastian muttered, trying to ignore what could only be jealousy flowing through his veins as Hector pulled his wife closer, leaned forward and whispered something in her ear.

Breanna laughed.

She was enjoying the moment. He was jealous.

Jealous. Such a dumb emotion considering the union he'd offered her. It might make sense if he'd held her close instead of taking that phone call. But he'd done as he had to and put Celiana first.

Now, he couldn't stop the worm from slinking down his veins. Breathe. He needed to breathe. The dance would be over soon.

Soon.

A few more couples ambled onto the dance floor, and Alessio offered his hand to his princess. "May I have this dance?"

"I thought you'd never ask." Briella placed her hand in her husband's but stopped before Sebastian. "Rather than standing here grumpy, you could always cut in."

"I just might." Sebastian raised his chin, enjoying the challenge in his sister-in-law's features before turning his attention back to his wife.

Breanna was enjoying herself. He wouldn't

steal that from her. But he would claim the next dance.

As soon as the song ended, he was by her side. "Do you mind?" He held out his hand, and his wife's fingers locked through his. His breath eased a little as she squeezed them.

"Your Majesty," Hector bent his head, then turned back to his queen. "I told you, Breanna. You owe me." He winked, then headed off the dance floor.

Sebastian tilted his head as his wife stepped into his arms. "Why do you owe him?"

"He bet me that you would interrupt either before the song finished or just after. I told him that was ridiculous, that you probably didn't even notice I was gone." She smiled, but her eyes didn't light up.

"Breanna." His fingers tightened on her back, pulling her a little closer. He bent his head, so his words were only for her. "I watched you the whole time. I knew exactly where you were. I wanted you for the next dance the moment you were on the floor."

And every dance after.

Breanna's smile was almost as bright as it had been for her friend. Almost. "I do hope you're happy. Hector wins a date night—"

"A date night?" The words came out harsher than he'd planned.

"Yes." She chuckled, though her features were

not as free as they were with Hector. "Dinner, though, I think we are making dinner? Not sure on the exact idea yet. But it is for a few hours in a couple of weeks or so. Again, the details are still a bit up in the air. I shall have to clear the schedules."

She enunciated the word *schedules* and he tried to find some way to figure out what it meant that his queen was going on a date with one of Celiana's most notorious playboys. The man's dance card was full, but he'd never courted a married woman. At least not openly.

"That will certainly make the headlines."

"I think that is Hector's plan." Breanna sighed as he pulled her a little closer. "The king and queen at his date night extravaganza or whatever he plans to call it."

"The king *and* queen." Sebastian blinked, and his footsteps faltered.

"Careful, you might step on my feet, and the lovely shoes Olga is crafting aren't here yet." This time her eyes lit up as she grinned at him.

The music slowed, and Sebastian closed the tiny amount of distance between them. "You knew what I was thinking, Your Highness." The sweet scent that was just Breanna infiltrated his nose.

"I did." She laid her head on his shoulder. They'd had one dance like this at their wedding, but his wife hadn't rested on him since. He hadn't known it was possible to miss something so much without realizing it.

The music lilted around them, and for a moment it was just the two of them in the world. His lips found her head. This wasn't what he'd promised her. But right now, he wanted so much more than a dutiful relationship.

"So, date night for some new venture for Hector. I think we can make that work." His lips brushed her hair again.

"I used to give Hector a hard time when we were in school together. Told him he couldn't settle on just one thing. He had to try everything. He skipped the traditional lemonade stand and started by selling a computer code that helped students do their math homework—according to Hector. Help the students cheat, was what our teachers said. That one nearly got him expelled. Then it was 3D printing and..." She shifted in his arms as the words failed to come to her.

He didn't loosen his grip, though if his wife stepped away, he wouldn't stop her.

Instead, she smiled at him. And his heart tripped in his chest.

"I can't remember. There have been so many. Hector has an idea. He chases it, and the rest of the world just seems to follow."

"We are alike in that way." Sebastian kissed the top of her head. He couldn't stop. He was drawn to this woman. A woman whose name he hadn't picked out of a hat. A woman he'd married just days after meeting her. A woman who should want more than him. Deserved more than him.

"No." Breanna pulled back as the music shifted. "Hector has ideas and he grows them into something. We have crowns that turn the eye."

There were no words to cut through that truth. Breanna didn't look sad or unhappy. It was acceptance on her features. Something he should be grateful for.

Instead, all he could think of was that the crown had stolen her ventures. Every single one of them.

The pop beat banged out, and Breanna laughed. Her hair bounced as lights hit her crown, her hips swaying to the beat. "Think you can keep up with these moves, Your Highness?"

"Of course." The heaviness around them parted. The worry retreating to the back of his mind. Pushed away, but never truly gone.

Breanna watched her husband's throat move and wanted to shake him. The man was exhausted. And yet, even here alone with his wife, he was swallowing his yawns. As if the image he presented could keep the exhaustion at bay.

"I might just fall into bed for the rest of the weekend." Breanna laughed as she stood in front of her door, hoping he might agree with her.

Smile at her like he had in his office this afternoon or on the dance floor an hour ago.

"If you need a break, we can schedule one. Not several days, but a day here and there."

She didn't bother to try to stop the rolling of her eyes. "Ooh, a whole day to myself. Wow." She put her hand on her chest, mostly to keep from shoving it into his shoulder.

"Breanna—" A yawn interrupted whatever diatribe he wanted to give her on duty.

"You are exhausted. What time do you get up? It seems to be a guarded secret." No matter who she asked, all she got was a shrug.

"Early." He leaned forward like he was going to drop a kiss on her lips.

Her breath caught. So many times over the last few days, she'd thought he wanted to kiss her. But he never followed through. And he didn't now.

Maybe she was the only one wanting kisses.

She crossed her arms, willing him to let her be a partner in more than just the public-facing activities of the court. Maybe they weren't like Briella and Alessio, but they could be more than strangers. Could be friends, at least. Even if her heart cried that it wanted more.

"I'm fine, Breanna."

"That wasn't the question I asked. And you aren't. You are exhausted. Let me help. It's why you wanted a queen. A partner. A person standing here." *Annie. Not me.* Though he hadn't wanted Annie either. Just a body. A person to stand there.

But she wasn't just going to stand there. "Sebastian…"

He let out a sigh, like he truly believed that this was his life and there was nothing more. "I'm fine." An edge hardened in his tone.

"I'm not sure you'd know if you weren't." Breanna raised her hand, cupping his cheek.

His face softened as he leaned into her. Rested himself on her palm. His breathing slowed, but he didn't let himself hold the position for long.

Far too soon, he raised himself, and the king stood fully before her. The mantle the only thing present now. "I would. I did. Last year. I broke. I lost myself. Alessio and then Briella took the hits. The press—" He cleared his throat, shaking his head and if he was trying to dash away the memories.

"The press was vile to Brie. But you are not responsible for that."

"I am. I was the one who was supposed to marry. It was my father's plan. A marriage, a union to make sure the Celiana royal love story he and my mother presented stayed true in the minds of the people. I refused. I wanted to take time to get to know the bride they'd selected. To try for a real union. Then Father passed, and Alessio stepped up with the princess lottery."

"They are fine now. They love each other." He

was in a way responsible for that. If he hadn't refused...

"Just because lightning struck for them does not take away that it should never have happened. I understand now what it means when I break and who it might hurt. Alessio, Brie. You."

"Sebastian."

He ignored her, pressing on, "I promise. I am fine."

It was a lie. But she didn't think he was saying it intentionally. No, her husband believed that he needed to break fully to be less than fine.

"Good night, Breanna. Rest well." Then he bowed and left her at her door.

The handle was cool in her hand as she watched his retreating form.

The Sebastian escorting her to her room was the king. Not the man who'd danced with her on the floor tonight. The man who'd smiled and held her close. The man she'd ached to kiss.

That man deserved freedom from the shackles of the other.

Her own yawn interrupted her thoughts. That was a question for a brain more awake than hers. A question for tomorrow.

There was a solution. Breanna just had to find it.

CHAPTER NINE

Today's agenda is quite full, Your Highness.

LETICIA, HER NEWLY hired assistant, always sent her text to arrive at one minute past midnight. It was the first thing she saw upon awaking. The reminder, as though she needed it, that she was the queen of Celiana.

Sebastian's partner...but only when it was the schedule.

Start time five past nine.

At least she'd managed to keep her schedule start time to nine in the weeks she'd been here. A boundary she'd had no luck getting her husband to follow through on.

Husband.

She'd set her alarm fifteen minutes earlier every day for the week. But even arriving in the kitchen at four fifty yesterday, she'd found only the hints of his presence. A freshly rinsed coffee mug, a note from him about the breakfast fixings he'd left for her in the fridge.

Did the man sleep?

If so, she'd yet to see evidence of it. That wasn't happening today though. They were having breakfast, talking, relaxing, and he wasn't starting his day until nine.

She'd even worked that in with Raul. Probably. Sebastian's assistant had agreed he needed a break and was willing to help. But she'd seen the underlying worry in his face.

So, assuming Raul was willing to follow through on the promise he'd made to the queen. Assuming she could figure out when he rose. Sebastian was resting today.

But that meant she had to catch him in the kitchen.

She looked at the watch he'd given her. Five past midnight. Blanket and pillow in hand, she was going to the kitchen.

One way or another, the king was going to spend a few hours with her today doing nothing.

"Breanna!"

The call was loud, but her brain was too mushy to truly capture the voice. She wrapped the blanket around her as cold seeped through her. Tired.

"Breanna!"

Kitchen, Sebastian, tired. All three words rattled in her mind before finally syncing. He was in the kitchen.

She popped up, looked at the clock through

bleary eyes and groaned. "Three thirty. Three thirty in the morning. What the hell, Sebastian?"

"I don't know what you mean. Why are you on the floor? With a pillow and blanket? How long have you been here?"

"Oh, no," Breanna pushed up on her elbow, stood, then pinched the bridge of her nose. Exhaustion gripped her, but she was not losing her train of thought. "I started the question session, so I get the first answer."

"There is no answer to, *'What the hell, Sebastian?'*"

Not true. There were many answers he might be able to give, if he just thought about it. "I think you know very well what I mean, Your Highness."

"You only call me that when you are frustrated. Do you want a cup of coffee?"

"No. Because it is bedtime. We should be asleep." Coffee at three thirty? *No, thank you.* "*You* should be asleep."

Her husband looked to the coffeepot, his fingers moving like he needed caffeine or he might lie down on the floor with her. "I've started my day at three for as long as I can remember."

That was heartbreaking.

"My father started at the same time. He woke me and we had coffee, then got on with the day." Sebastian started towards the coffeepot, not managing to cover his yawn. The only thing keeping the man running was routine.

"At what age?" She grabbed his hand; he was not going to start the coffeepot. Not right now.

"Huh?" He looked at her hand around his wrist, then back at her. "It's fine, Breanna."

No, it very much was not!

"At what age?" She'd repeat the question as many times as necessary to get an answer.

He started to push a hand through his already done hair, but caught himself. Even at three thirty in the blasted morning, the man didn't want to ruffle the king's appearance. "I don't know. Sometime around ten or eleven, I guess. The crown—"

She tightened her grip on his wrist. "If you are about to say the crown does not rest, I swear…" Her parents were controlling. They believed their daughters belonged to them. It was horrifying. Sebastian's father had convinced him that he belonged to an entire country.

She pulled on his hand. "We are going back to bed."

The words were out, and she heard exactly how they sounded. "Not like that, though!"

"Breanna—" His voice was soft, low, and despite the exhaustion pulling through her, she wanted to lean into him. Kiss away his frowns and make him believe he was worth more than what his title gave him.

The man was her husband. He was also a work-aholic and still a near-stranger. "Do not *Breanna* me. You need sleep. *I* need sleep."

"I don't." He used his free hand to cover his mouth as another yawn escaped.

If only there were a way to reach into the afterlife. Because Breanna very much wanted to have a discussion with King Cedric. At least his mother was still within her reach. Because this was ridiculous.

But getting angry right now was not going to solve anything.

"I'll make you a deal. You lie in my bed for fifteen minutes." She grabbed her phone, opened the clock app and put it on a fifteen-minute timer. "I will start this the second your head hits the pillow and you close your eyes. If you are still awake when the alarm goes off, I will not stop you from starting your day when others are stumbling home from the bar."

"You're tired." Sebastian lay his hand over hers on his wrist.

"I *am* exhausted. And I had to sleep on the kitchen floor to even find out what time *my husband* wakes. So yes. I am exhausted and a little furious."

"At me?" For a moment he looked so young. So lost. So much like the boy he must have been when King Cedric dragged him from bed, plied him with coffee and told him his soul belonged to a kingdom.

Breanna stepped close and shook her head. "No. I am furious at your father. But we can discuss that in a few hours. Right now, we are both running on fumes."

"I'm used to it." He grinned, and the twinkle in his eye would have been adorable if she didn't think it was wholly tiredness pulling at him.

"Then lying down for fifteen minutes will not cause a problem."

He looked at the coffeepot. "Let me set it up." He moved fast, his hands flying in an easy motion that he'd done thousands of times.

The drip started. She pulled on him. "Now."

He looked at her and then the coffeepot. "At least the coffee will be here when I get back." He dropped a quick kiss on her nose, surprise dotting his features as he pulled back. "Right. Fifteen minutes, Breanna."

"Fifteen minutes, Sebastian. From the time you close your eyes!"

Bending down, he collected her pillow and blanket and nodded towards the door. "After you, Your Highness." His gaze was bright.

Maybe she was wrong. Maybe he wasn't as exhausted as she thought. Well, then her alarm would go off and she'd find some other way to get the king to relax.

Opening the door to her suite, she took a deep

breath as her bed came into view. This was mostly a spontaneous plan. She wanted him to take a break, but she'd not truly expected to find him up so early. And now they were in her bedroom.

Sebastian put the pillow on the bed and crawled in. "The timer starts the moment my head touches the pillow."

"When you close your eyes." She'd been a child who hated bedtime. She knew the tricks to staying awake. And she suspected Sebastian did, too. For very different reasons.

"You coming to bed, too? You're exhausted."

"If I lie down, I will fall asleep. And then the alarm will go off and wake us both."

"I will still be up in fifteen minutes." So sure of himself.

"Then me sitting in this chair doesn't cause a problem." Breanna raised her chin. The king was stubborn, but she could rise to the occasion, too.

"Fine." He lay down, let out a sigh, then closed his eyes.

Breanna started the timer. And shut it off at the four-minute mark when Sebastian's light snores echoed across her chamber.

The man needed rest. And if no one else was going to get it for him, then she would. She sent a quick note to Raul clearing his schedule for the morning. Then Breanna stepped beside the bed.

The lines around his eyes were gone. He looked

peaceful. A stray piece of hair fell across his face, but she dared not touch him.

"Good night, Sebastian." Breanna's words were more in her head than spoken. She grabbed a blanket, curled up in the oversized chair, closing her eyes, and let sleep take her, too.

Sebastian knew as he rolled over that the fifteen minutes had passed long ago. He rubbed the back of his hand against his head, then looked at his wrist. His watch was gone.

No. He blinked. He put it on every morning, first thing. It was part of the routine his father had kept. And Sebastian kept. Bed at eleven, up at three. Clothes already set out. Watch on the dresser.

Sitting up, he looked to the window. But the heavy curtains were pulled, giving no indication of the time. How long had he been out? What meetings had he missed? How far behind schedule was he?

Rolling out of bed, Sebastian reached his hands up, stretching. He needed to get moving, but he couldn't argue that he didn't feel great. Apparently, his body craved the nap.

Walking into his wife's study, he wasn't surprised to see her standing next to her workbench. The woman seemed glued to that space when she wasn't on official business.

"Are you feeling rested?" Breanna set her tools

down and smiled at him. A full smile. Like the one he'd seen her give Hector. But this was directed at him because she'd won the bet.

It was like winning the lottery. His whole body seemed to sing as her smile radiated over him.

"I am. Feel free to say told you so." Sebastian had earned the call-out. He must have been completely out for her to remove his watch without him noticing.

Her dark curls bounced as she tilted her head. "Why would I say told you so?"

He waited for the laughter, or some other trick. That had been Sam's go-to. A laugh to lighten the mood before a devastating comment. She'd excelled at weaponized words.

Something he'd only realized after their terrible breakup.

Breanna looked at him as he waited for the shoe to fall. Better to get it over with than for it to fall later when he wasn't expecting it. "It's okay. I earned it."

"Why did you earn it?" Such a simple question.

He'd failed today. For the first time in more than a year, he'd missed meetings and caused havoc. All because he couldn't operate as well exhausted.

"Because you were right." His father was always right. And his mother. Hell, even Alessio stepped in after his father's passing when Sebastian had fallen apart and made all the right choices.

King Cedric had made it look easy. His mother was excellent at navigating aristocratic politics, and Alessio had come home from abroad and stepped right into the hole Sebastian had vacated.

He'd been raised for this life. Trained— literally at dawn. Yet he was constantly feeling like he was failing. Living up to his father's legacy was draining.

"It's not about being right. It's about taking care of people."

Taking care of people. That sounded nice. But it was his job. He took care of Celiana. He didn't need anyone looking after him.

"Yes, you do."

Breanna words made his head pop back. "What?"

"You were thinking that you don't need anyone looking after you." She crossed her arms; her bright gaze bore into him. "I can see it written on your face."

"I am the king, and we…" He gestured to the space between them. "We are married, but…"

So many things hung on that *but*.

His wife's stance softened. "Even when the marriage is nothing more than a contract agreement."

She took a deep breath, closing her eyes. Did she want more? Was that even possible? Would hoping for it destroy him if he was wrong?

Yes.

"Breanna." He wasn't sure what to say. No words came to his well-rested mind.

"You slept for nearly twelve hours. Do you know how exhausted you have to be to do that?" She moved around the sewing table and stepped right in front of him.

"Twelve hours?" His brain was firing, but it couldn't seem to calculate everything that meant.

Breanna put her hand on his chest. The motion was soft, but he got the distinct feeling that she'd shove him if he fought her right now. "The entire weight of this country does not rest on you, Sebastian. And even *if* it did, you still deserve some rest."

His hand lay over hers and he leaned his head against hers. This was a lot to take in. There were meetings to reschedule, but right now all he could muster was, "Thank you."

"You're welcome. But, um…" Color traveled up her neck as she pulled back a little. "There is more. I…um…"

"You are saying 'um' a lot." Sebastian let out a chuckle.

"I cleared your schedule for the next two weeks." The words were said so fast he almost didn't catch them.

"That is a funny joke." He laughed, and then the chuckles just kept coming. Two weeks. Tears of mirth started down his cheeks. Two weeks off as the king. Sure.

She might as well as said that they were going to the moon tomorrow. It was as feasible.

"I did." Breanna stepped away, and he ached to pull her back.

"Breanna, two weeks? I'm the king. You are the queen."

"Thanks for the reminder. If we were a normal couple, a two-week honeymoon would be a luxury, but it would raise no eyebrows. This is the same."

"Honeymoon?" The word hit his heart and the simple meaning behind it. Honeymoon. Something nearly every couple took. Something he hadn't even thought of. "I didn't think—"

"Of a honeymoon for us. Yeah. I know." She focused on the fabric on the table, not quite covering her sigh.

Darn it.

He'd hurt her. Not intentionally, but that perception was what mattered, not intent. Rule one you learned in the palace.

"Did you want a honeymoon?" He'd assumed she wanted the crown. Assumed she'd beaten her sister for it. Assumed that he was just an accessory.

Assumed a lot, if he was honest with himself.

"What I want stopped mattering long ago. If it ever did." Breanna grabbed the shears and trimmed an edge.

If it ever did.

"You didn't really want to be queen, did you?" He'd suspected it after their wedding. Worried over it. But he wanted her to say it. Though he had no idea what he'd do with the information.

The scissors in her hand seemed to slip just a bit. "What are you going to do with two weeks off, Your Highness? I suspect it is your first vacation."

Deflecting the question. Breanna was nearly as skilled at shifting the topic as him. But right now, he didn't have time to force the issue.

"I don't know." Right now, he needed to talk to Raul about scheduling their honeymoon. If he had two weeks off, they were not hiding away in the palace. He could at least give his bride a vacation.

CHAPTER TEN

"WHERE ARE YOU going on your honeymoon?" Annie's peppy voice was a good sign. It was the first time she'd sounded like herself since she'd fled their parents' mansion.

"It's just a story for the press, Annie." One she'd cooked up as she'd watched her husband sleep soundly. It had taken her longer to convince Raul to leak the news to the press. The man was as on board with Sebastian taking a rest as her. Maybe more so, but he was also steeled in tradition and protocol.

Only her promise to post it on a piece of paper on the palace wall if that was the only way to accomplish it had caused him to bend. She'd approved the press release from the public relations office then waited…and waited…for Sebastian to wake.

And she'd not seen him since he'd left her room after she told him about the two-week vacation yesterday. Their first fight. Though it didn't have much bite behind it. For fights to matter, you had to matter.

She was a name not drawn out of a hat. A woman to wear the crown. One easily overtaken by a phone call.

Breanna blew out a breath. As much as she'd love to soak up the sun on a beach, read a fun novel and think of nothing, she had no illusion that they'd go anywhere. Though Breanna planned to get to know her husband during this forced isolation period.

If he didn't have work to focus on, then he could focus on her for at least a few minutes. Right? They could have a real conversation. Not one timed to fit into his always busy schedule. Not one easily interrupted by nonsense masquerading as emergency.

"A story, Breanna." The disappointment flowed through the phone connection.

Disappointing her parents was a common thing; disappointing Annie always cut. But letting her sister know how much she wished there was some truth to the story was not an option.

They weren't a real couple, but she wished he wanted to spend time with her. It shouldn't matter. Her family had never spent much time with Breanna. The bonus twin. The one who meant her parents got a two-for-one deal.

She'd survived by pretending, accepting, and finding the silver lining.

And it was going to be her life forever. That was the part that stung. The knowledge that she'd never have the fairy tale. Not that the fairy tale truly existed.

"Well, in your mind you can imagine me in a bikini on the beach, reading a sex-filled romance novel while the sun kisses my skin."

She heard a noise and turned to find her husband standing at her door. His head was bent over his phone. Had he heard her? Probably not. The man was focused on whatever was on the screen, not her.

"I need to go, Annie. I want to see pictures of the changes you made to the apartment when you get a chance." Her sister had cut a deal with the apartment manager. He'd pay for supplies, and she could upgrade her unit and the three empty ones. It would let him raise the price of rent and give her a start on replacing her portfolio. It was a brilliant idea.

And one Annie had come up with on her own. Her sister was getting her freedom. That was worth everything. Even marriage to a king she still didn't really know after weeks of being his wife.

"Good afternoon, Sebastian." The small line that appeared on his cheek when he was trying to hide a frown stood out. "I suspect you are here about the honeymoon story."

"I admit that it surprised me to find my queen has already managed to get the staff on her side." The words were said with a little bite. Surely he knew the staff was looking out for him, too. They were all worried about him—if only he could see that they cared about him. Not the crown.

Breanna plastered on the smile she'd used at home far too often. "It was a good plan, though. Right?" She was actually pretty proud of the calculation.

"It was." He looked at his watch. "You have thirty minutes to pack."

"Pack?" Breanna laughed. Was he kicking her out? Just for making him take a vacation.

"Yes. Pack. For the beach. Make sure you put the bikini in."

"Bikini?" He had heard her. He wasn't focused elsewhere. Was this a joke? A way to poke fun at a queen who'd overstepped her place?

Sebastian tapped his wrist "Twenty-eight minutes, Breanna."

"Where are we going?" How was she supposed to pack if she didn't know what was expected?

"On a honeymoon." Sebastian winked, then headed for the door. "I need to change something in my bag." He hit his watch one more time. "Twenty-seven minutes," he chuckled as he closed the door.

Checkmate.

* * *

His wife had successfully found a way to make him take two weeks off. Releasing the honeymoon statement while he was still deep in the land of Nod was a stroke of genius. And a honeymoon was a good idea.

It wouldn't be traditional. No matter how many times his wife appeared in his dreams, how many times he replayed the kiss on their wedding day. The dances they shared. The laughter in those stolen minutes. The feel of her while she was pressed against him.

He'd sworn to have a marriage of convenience. To give her a life with no expectations of sharing a bed with man who'd chosen her sister's name from a hat.

But they were going on a honeymoon. A long-overdue extended get-to-know-you session. His plans to head to the mountains to ski had changed as soon as he'd heard her chattering with her sister.

"Imagine me in a bikini."

It was all too easy for him to piece together the image. His mouth had watered. Spending two weeks with Breanna on the sand wearing a hopefully skimpy bathing suit would be its own form of torture.

That would have been enough of a reason for him to text Raul to change the location for this trip, but the wistfulness in her voice had stolen away his breath. The hint of wanting something. He knew that sound, the plea only his heart recognized.

She'd said that to the one person she trusted. Her sister.

"What I want stopped mattering long ago—if it ever did."

He loved skiing. The few day trips he'd managed to make as a child and teen were heaven. During his year of rebellion, Sebastian had spent more time on the slopes than at the palace.

But if her first choice was the beach? Well, she was the one who'd plotted this honeymoon out. It should be her choice.

Breanna walked up the hallway with a backpack and a small carry-on rolling bag.

"Where is the rest of your luggage?" His mother went on an overnight with more luggage than Breanna had on her.

She looked at the roller, then back at him. "You said pack for the beach. Bathing suits and shorts don't take up that much room."

His mouth watered, and he had to take a breath before he could answer. Control. His wife was gorgeous, and the idea of spending two weeks with her barely clothed...

Focus.

They could always purchase items if she needed them. The benefits of royal life.

"I do need to stop by a bookstore." Breanna smiled. "I am all out of—"

The pause hung in the air. He'd heard her words to Annie. All of them.

"Sex-filled novels?" Sebastian winked. The idea of his wife reading such novels was its own turn-on.

"Yes." She didn't look away. No color crept up her cheeks. Good. This wasn't something that should embarrass her.

"Do you know what you want?" Sebastian pulled up his phone. They could order whatever she wanted and have it sent to the beach cottage. It would be there, wrapped in nice packaging before they arrived.

Her fingers wrapped around his wrist, and she pulled his phone from his hand. The touch was gone before his mind could fully register it, but the heat it left behind scorched his skin.

"I have my TBR on a website dedicated to books. But that isn't the same as a shop."

"TBR?" Sebastian read occasionally, but he wasn't aware of a specialized lingo in the reading community.

"To be read pile." Breanna shook her head with a vigor that screamed, *How can you not know that?* "Mine is infinitely long, but I will always add to it."

"So, pick a few things off of it." Sebastian started to reach for his phone again but stopped.

There was wonder in her eye. A look that was purely Breanna.

Have I ever looked like that? Excited? Free? No thought of the place or the crown.

He knew the answer. And the fact that time would likely steal the excitement from the woman in front of him tore through him.

"The fun of book shopping is the store. Walking down the aisle, picking up something with a fun cover or great title. You don't know what you want until it calls to you from the shelf." Breanna was nearly bouncing. "I know we are royals and everything, but surely there is a way we can stop at a store?"

Now she was bouncing. "You might even find something to keep you busy this week. Something besides work correspondence!" Her face was bright and excited.

And he was about to crush it with reality.

"As you say, we are royals. You are the queen. Stepping into a shop isn't as simple as just stepping into a shop."

Her face shifted, "I understand, but I mean, I am also…" Her voice wobbled. Then she lifted her chin. "We have to have a process for doing so. When you go…"

He watched the wheels turn and the realization cross her face. "I don't go anywhere that isn't preplanned. Everything is controlled, and nothing is ever just for fun. It's to promote a shop or raise awareness of a cause."

"Duty thy name is Sebastian." Breanna pulled at her neck, then reached for her phone. "I guess the TBR list it is." The laugh that fell from her lips wasn't crisp. It wasn't fun or happy.

Resigned.

That was the word for Breanna in this moment. Resigned. No anger. No frustration

She pulled up an app, clearing her throat. "I guess the top five on here are a good start."

He took a screen shot of the top ten and sent it to Raul with instructions for them to be delivered to the beach house before them.

"Wonderful." He pointed to her bag. "Really sure you don't need to add anything else? We're going for two weeks."

"Really."

All right then. He held out a hand, his body relaxing as her hand fit into his. "Time for a honeymoon."

Whatever that means.

The blue bikini was skimpier than she remembered. All of the bathing suits Breanna had brought were skimpier than she remembered. Annie used to joke that Breanna bought as little material as possible as though that would let her soak up more sun.

Which was technically true. And if this was

a traditional honeymoon, the bright blue string bikini—well, this would make most people's mouth water.

He'd told her that he'd watched her with Hector. Hector swore Sebastian was jealous. But how could he be?

Breanna was hoping for kisses. Sitting in his lap like a fool, only to have the phone give her husband a reason to be free of her. Oh, he'd offered five minutes, but she hadn't wanted that. No matter how many times she thought he was about to drop his lips to hers, the most he ever did was lightly kiss her head. A sweet motion for those watching, probably.

And on their "honeymoon," they had separate rooms.

"Technically, I don't have anything with more coverage." She looked at her bed and sighed. There was no way she was spending this vacation inside.

In my own room.

She opened the door to her private beach entrance, pushing back the tears that were pulling at her. A private room. A private entrance. All to herself...on a honeymoon.

If she gave herself time to think on that, her heart might break. Silver lining, Breanna. She was on the beach. She was away from the palace. Away from the schedule.

The sun hit her face, and Breanna's heart lifted

a little. The beach called to her. She had a book—freshly delivered—and a lounge chair calling her name.

Strolling up to the chairs, she was shocked to find Sebastian already in his. Washboard abs ordinarily hidden by suits and tailored shirts were on full display. He looked like a man who had stepped from the pages of one of her books.

Maybe being around her hot, mostly unclothed husband for two weeks wasn't the best plan.

"It's nice out, but the sun is bright. If you want me to get the umbrella—" Sebastian turned his head, his words stopping as he stared at her.

Guess the bikini was as head-turning as she thought.

"I like the sun. Annie says I crave it." It was one way they were different. Annie liked cloudy, rainy days.

"My parents could always tell us apart in the summer because I had a tan." It was the only time in the year the girls weren't interchangeable.

"Only in the summer?"

Her husband's tone was sharp, but she just shrugged. Mistaking their daughters' names never bothered their parents—if it bothered the girls, then that was their problem.

"Identical twins. Interchangeable and all."

His hand was on hers in an instant. "You are not interchangeable."

"Sure I am. Even on the day you came looking

for Annie I was. It's okay." Mostly it was. It was her life.

Sebastian's thumb ran along her wrist, the movement sending little spikes of energy up her arms. "I am glad you were the one who came into that room, Breanna."

Her name rumbled from his lips. Her name. Not her title. His muscles were relaxed, but her eyes couldn't seem to stop from staring. What would it feel like to run her hands down them? Drag her lips across them?

Not like she'd find out in the private room she occupied. He was glad it was her. He was holding her hand, but not pulling her any closer.

Get it together.

Breanna slid onto the chair next to his and pushed her sunglasses back on her head. Time for some sun, and she didn't want to risk tan lines around her eyes with the glasses. That and forcing her eyes closed would make sure she couldn't drool over the physical attributes of her husband.

"Annie is the one who stands out—even looking just like me."

"What is that supposed to mean?" Sebastian shifted beside her. Maybe pushing up on his elbow? If she was sitting on the other side, she could get a great view of his butt. Of course, if her chair was on that side, he would have turned to look at her that way. So, the hypothetical situation where she drooled over his backside was flawed from inception.

She heard him twist again but didn't open her eyes. "It means what it sounds like it means." Breanna wasn't sure what the question was about. And her mind had very little available space for anything more than picturing her hot husband who she'd barely touched during their month together.

Seriously, fantasizing about how to get a glimpse of the Adonis's butt. Yep. There was no way she was daring to open her eyes. At least with the sun's rays dancing on her skin, she could pretend the heat wasn't embarrassment crawling up her body.

Sebastian's hand stroked her arm, and she nearly shot up. Only a lifetime of ignoring her wants kept her in place.

"Breanna." Her name was soft as he rubbed a thumb across her arm.

Goose bumps appeared despite the heat.

"Breanna."

"Yes, Sebastian?"

He waited for a moment. Probably seeing if she'd open her eyes. Nope, not happening.

"Why does Annie stand out?" The words were barely above a whisper.

Why was this the first conversation they were having? It was sunny. They could talk of books. Of places they'd visited. Him for official business. Her for family business trips. They could talk about anything. But no, he wanted to know this.

If she didn't answer, he'd press. She knew that. But right now, it was a soft question. A plea. "Annie was the daughter to secure a good marriage. I was the extra. A two-for-one deal, they liked to say. And she is so talented. She is going to make a name for herself. All for herself."

Sebastian didn't say anything, but the pressure on her hand increased.

She hadn't meant to say anything else, but now that the first words were out, her mouth seemed incapable of controlling itself. She'd never told anyone how it felt to be the extra. How much she wanted a different life.

She'd wanted to teach. To disappear into a classroom. Educate the next generation. Something so small. Meaningless to her parents. So meaningless they'd stymied every attempt she'd made to get into the classroom.

"And you?"

If she opened her eyes, the words would likely stop. She'd lose the ability to form them. But she'd also have to see the pity in Sebastian's eyes.

"My dreams were smaller. A classroom decorated with bright colors and little students who wanted to be in circle time. Or didn't. At that age, sitting still is not a skill most little ones have. My student teaching days were my happiest. But teaching is not a profession for Galanis women. Not when we can marry well, according to my parents."

She laughed, but the lack of humor wasn't lost on her. "Anyways, Annie is brilliant with colors. She has dreams. She's an interior designer. One day everyone on this island will know exactly who she is—for her work—not her name."

"So when I pulled her name from the hat…" Sebastian's whispers chilled her skin.

"She was going to marry you. I saw it. All the work she'd done to get her portfolio ready. Our escape hatch." She cleared her throat. "Anyways, I pointed out that you didn't know her so you couldn't mind if we switched the script. We look the same, after all. And you didn't know us. Which was true."

"Breanna." Her name. The twin he hadn't meant to meet at the altar. Why was this bothering her now? They'd been married a month. A month as his queen. A month of accepting that this was her life.

And she was doing a good job. Or she had been. Until she'd stepped onto this beach.

"I don't say that to make you feel bad. I say it as the truth. Annie has a dream." Breanna sighed as she remembered the first room Annie had ever redecorated. A spare room her mother had no use for. A room designed for failure.

Her parents had only let Annie try because

Breanna would not stop pestering. And then the finished product was gorgeous. It was still the room her mother had all the guests sleep in. Not that they'd ever praised Annie.

But others would.

"And your dream was a classroom?"

Rolling over, she opened her eyes, letting the grin swimming in her soul appear freely. "No. My dream was for Annie to get her dream. And she is going to. She has an apartment now. She is decorating it, and the empty units, with her landlord's approval. Maybe it isn't the fancy portfolio our parents stole, but it's something that can't be taken from her."

"But what was *your* dream?" Sebastian's hand gripped hers. Heat bloomed beneath it.

She lifted it, placed a soft kiss on it, then rolled onto her back. "That was my dream. Now my dream is to get some sun." There was no point discussing this. She'd made her choice.

This was her life now. She was a queen. Annie was free.

Maybe this wasn't the life she'd envisioned. She'd never step into the classroom as a teacher. Never see little eyes light up as they learned their letters and numbers. But she'd make the same choice again without question.

CHAPTER ELEVEN

"Want to order some lunch?" Breanna stretched on the lounge chair next to him. She'd occupied it nearly every moment since they'd arrived yesterday. Flipping when the timer on her phone went off. Or running into the sea for a quick dip. "Or would you rather cook?"

The sun kissed her skin in ways he could only dream of.

"What would you prefer?" He had a fully stocked kitchen here. Outside of sushi, he could fix up just about anything she requested.

His wife sat up. The pink polka-dot string bikini left so little to the imagination, if he was standing, he might drop to his knees in worship of the beauty beside him. She was delectable.

The blue bikini from yesterday had played the main role in his dreams last night. Today, his fingers ached to travel down her stomach. Circle her belly button, see what sounds she might make if his lips followed the same path.

None of which was going to happen.

"I do not enjoy cooking, so fixing my own food on vacation is not high on my priorities." Breanna moved her hand like she was going to push his shoulder, but he caught it and held it.

Her eyes flicked to their combined fingers, but she didn't pull back. "However, you do enjoy it. And this is your vacation. Do you want to cook?"

She'd put his needs first. Again. It was a pattern that he should have seen faster. One he might have seen if he'd spent more time with his queen. The woman put others first. It was an admirable quality.

But it didn't mean you had to give up everything you wanted. Outside of sewing, did his wife even know what her preferences were? Had she ever had dreams that revolved just around her?

Just because she was an identical twin didn't mean she didn't get to be an individual.

"What is your favorite food? The day after our wedding, you asked about me, but I learned little other than you like a little coffee with your syrup in the morning." Her laughter filled his heart as she swung their combined hands.

"My coffee is not that full of syrup." She stuck her tongue out, then laughed.

His statement wasn't that far from the truth. His wife put at least four squirts of coffee syrup in each mug. He watched her create combinations that he'd never consider. Sometimes it was clear she had a drink she was recreating. Other times it seemed she was just flying by the seat of her sweet tooth.

"What is your favorite food, Breanna? I know you like lemon cake, and I will make that if you like, but one cannot live on dessert alone."

"Not sure that is true." Breanna pulled her hand back, and even though he wanted to reach for it again, Sebastian let it be.

"I can't make it if I don't know it." This was such a simple question. One most people could spout off with no thought.

"I like vegetable lasagna. Our cook used to make it once a week so I had something besides salads for dinner." She rolled her head, shifting in the chair. Discomfort was clear on her features.

This was about food; it wasn't hard. Or it shouldn't be. And the statement's meaning struck him. "Did you not have vegetarian options at dinner?" The Galanis estate was famous for the luxury dinners they served investors. Sebastian had attended more than one event at the estate with his father.

He racked his memory for anything about those events, but they were a blur in a lifetime of service. He wasn't even sure he'd seen Breanna and Annie there. Though they were probably in the sea of people.

"My parents did not support my choice." She stood and walked towards the sea.

He followed.

"That can't be surprising, Sebastian. Unless you and Raul had intervened, I would have eaten very little at my own wedding reception." She strolled into the waves, then turned and splashed him.

Water dripped down his face as she squealed and sent another small wave towards him. He cupped some water and tossed it her way. Her laughter increased.

The moment was fun, and happy. A honeymoon moment—and once more she'd redirected the conversation away from her. He splashed some more water her way, then reached for her waist and pulled her towards him. "What is your favorite food, Breanna? I am not letting you go until you tell me." Sebastian dipped his head and kissed her forehead.

He'd done that many times. It was never thought out, and not what he truly wanted, but he didn't want to push her for more than she'd signed on for. Even if he craved more.

Water slipped off his wife's face, and she didn't pull away from him. Instead, her hips pressed against him as the waves broke around them.

"You plan to hold me until I tell you my favorite food, Sebastian?" His wife moved her head, her lips so close to his. "Not sure that is much of a threat."

The sun's heat had nothing on the flames pouring through him. Steam should have risen from the ocean water as his mind replayed Breanna's comments back to him. "Breanna." His brain seemed incapable of forming any other thought besides his wife's name.

"Sebastian." Her arms wrapped around his neck. "How long do you think we'll just stand here? High tide comes in shortly. Then what?"

"What if I cut you a deal?" He stroked her back, enjoying the feel of her in his arms.

"A deal?" Her arms tightened just a little, and her hips brushed his again. The sun glinted off her dark hair. It was like he was standing with a fairy-tale creature. One he desperately wanted answers from. Though the question was far too simple for a fairy tale.

"Sebastian." Her purr echoed with the waves.

Maintaining his focus was a never-ending battle. "A deal." He cleared his throat, the action doing nothing to clear the thoughts of trailing his lips down her throat. "You tell me your favorite dish; I fix it. Then we spend the night cuddled on the couch. You pick the movie."

"I told you." She pressed her lips to his. The connection lasted barely a second. "Veggie lasagna."

"No. You said the cook made that once a week so you didn't have to eat salads. Not the same thing. And if you shrug that off—"

"You'll what? Kiss me into submission?"

Tempting. Oh, so very tempting. And if he

didn't think she was using this to make him try to forget about herself, then he might just offer that. But this was important.

Even if she didn't think so.

"I won't cuddle on the couch." He wasn't sure how they'd slipped from serious conversations to playfulness, but he was embracing it. There was more than one way to get an answer. And sometimes humor worked best of all.

The Sebastian he'd been a year ago bolted from the cage he'd locked him away in. "Or maybe I will spend the whole movie talking. Just interrupting and asking questions."

"You wouldn't." She threw one hand over her heart in playful surrender, but the other stayed wrapped around his neck.

"I guess I don't know. I ate a lot of salads, so definitely not that. At home it was lasagna though…my college roommate, Binna, used to make this potato dish. It…" She closed her eyes.

This was a moment he recognized. A dish that touched you. That made you feel something. It was something chefs worked for years to achieve. He'd once made a lamb stew that had brought tears to his eyes as the flavors mixed together.

Food had power. It held memories…good and bad.

"Describe it to me." He whispered the words against her ear as the water rose around them, binding them together. His fingers stroked her back. Staying a respectful distance from the top of her bikini bottom.

She brushed her lips against his, again. It was like they were going with the motions. This place was out of time and space. Just for them.

"Breanna." Her name was power. He ached for her to deepen the kiss, but he wasn't going to push this.

"Sebastian." Her lips passed his again. Then she seemed to remember they'd been talking about food.

"Binna used a giant pot with a lid. Not a sauce pot but something she'd brought over from Korea. But you could find it anywhere. She joked with me once that I knew so little about cooking, I thought the pot was something special. She had a name for it, but one of the other roommates called it an oven of some kind."

"A Dutch oven." It wasn't an uncommon method for making a stew. In fact, he'd crafted several in the one he stored in his kitchen.

"Yep. That's it. Binna's dish was called gochu-jang potato stew. I have no idea what the recipe was, and I wish I'd asked. Unfortunately, we lost touch after graduation. I heard she works at some big pharmaceutical firm in Germany now. The spices were strong, and I remember she was worried the scent would upset people."

"Did it?" Food was home. It was also something people judged. At uni, a young man had talked about how the kids at his school bullied him for the ethnic food his mother packed each day. A reminder of home for her. Something that made him different during a period everyone wanted to fit in.

Now he owned one the most successful restaurants on the island, and people paid a good bit for the Vietnamese cuisine others had judged.

Breanna shook her head. "It drove them to our door, but in a good way. It was so aromatic and yummy. Whenever people smelled it, we'd have them begging for a taste. I think Binna could have funded university by selling the stew."

"Well, I know how to make a gochujang stew, so I just need to see if there is gochujang in the spice cabinet here. I keep it in my kitchen at the palace. I'm not sure I have the exact potatoes Binna used, but it is a fairly standard dish, so we can play around and see if we can recreate it."

"Seriously?" Breanna planted a solid kiss on his lips before pulling back. "Oh."

It looked like all the blood in her body might be running to her face. "You're turning red." Sebastian dropped a playful kiss on her nose. "Don't want my bride getting sunburned."

"It has nothing to do with the sun, Your Highness." Breanna kissed his nose, recreating the movement he'd used.

He held his breath, and when her lips met his this time, there was no hesitation. A strong wave pushed against them, and rather than pull back, she wrapped her legs around his waist.

She opened her mouth, her tongue sweeping his, and the world melted away. She tasted of the ocean, sun and future. Breanna. His wife. His queen.

The kiss was over far too soon. She dipped her head, then grabbed his hand and pulled him towards the beach. "Let's see if you have the spice."

If perfection ever needed a new descriptor, it could use this moment to build it. He wanted to stop time. Be just Sebastian and Breanna forever.

Spices and ocean air might be her new favorite scent. She had no idea how she'd recreate it, but the spice smell meant she wasn't surprised to find Sebastian standing in the kitchen tossing a few things into the Dutch oven he'd found in the back of a cabinet yesterday.

"I figured we'd eat leftovers today." They had at least enough stew for a second serving. His gochujang potato stew wasn't the same as Binna's, but it was good. And the fact that he'd made something for her, something she wanted… it was a feeling she couldn't describe.

Which was why she'd jumped into his arms yesterday. And kissed him. It was spontaneous. But it felt right. Like she'd been waiting her whole life for a switch that was finally on. He'd kissed her back. Really kissed her.

Maybe he'd finally initiate a kiss. A real one instead of brushes against her forehead and nose. Their relationship was finally shifting.

Relationship. She wanted to laugh at the word. They'd gone from married strangers to people who'd shared a confidence beside the sea. It should feel awkward.

Should feel weird. They were married. Staying in separate rooms. But kissing and touching and…and figuring out what they were. It was certainly a unique way for spouses to play get-to-know-you.

Still, it felt right.

"We can have the stew for lunch. But I'm making some lentil curry for dinner. It will be perfect after cooking all day." Sebastian tilted his head towards the coffee. "I just made a fresh pot."

Just made.

"How long have you been up?" These two weeks were supposed to be about him resting. He couldn't do that if he was rising at three.

Sebastian bent his head.

The sudden focus on a dish she guessed he'd made dozens of times and the rapid spin of the spoon broke her heart. "Sebastian." He'd spent his entire life in service. Even on vacation, he was still serving. Except instead of a country, it was a focus of one. But what about what he wanted? What he needed?

She walked up behind him, wrapping her arms

around his waist. She laid her head against shoulder. "What time, honey?"

The endearment slipped out, but she wasn't going to focus on that now. They were helping each other. Giving each other rest. A place away from the lives they'd grown up in. A fresh start, hopefully.

"I managed to stay in bed until five."

Managed...

"Okay. But what time did you wake up?" She was a master of wording, too. One did not grow up in the Galanis household without learning more than a few phrasing tricks.

He chuckled, but there was no humor in the sound. "My wife is keen to my tricks already. I thought that was something that took time to develop in a marriage."

She squeezed him tighter. There was no judgment here. Just concern. "Sebastian."

"Three forty-five." He uttered the time and shrugged against her. "It's like my body needs to be up and going."

His voice was coated in exhaustion and frustration. "Sorry."

"You don't have to be sorry." His body was following the only routine it had ever known. The routine that had been forced onto him as a child. She couldn't get mad at that. At least not at him.

He stirred the dish, but she didn't let go. She was here for him. "During my rebellious year, I used to slip my security early in the morning. It drove Alessio mad. He accused me of trying to get hurt. Brie gave me an exceptionally strong talking-to one day. Told me I was hurting him."

And that would have nearly killed him. Sebastian cared for everyone. Full stop.

"Anyways, even when I was pushing back on the duty I was born for, I couldn't manage to keep myself in bed. What kind of rebellion involves being up before the dawn?"

"Not a very good one." She kissed his shoulder. "Somehow, I can't imagine you as rebellious. I mean, I remember that year. I know you call it failure and other ridiculous things, but please!"

Sebastian turned in her arms, wrapping his arms around her waist. They stood there, in the kitchen. His lips pressed to her head. "And what would you know about rebellion, Breanna?"

"Oh." She pulled back, then kissed his cheek. "I have rebelled a time or two." She laughed and kissed his shoulder again.

"I doubt that, very seriously, *Your Highness.*" This time his chuckle had a true lilt of humor.

She pushed on his shoulder, breaking the connection and offering a very fake pout. "How dare you say that." She grabbed a mug of coffee, dropped four pumps of brown sugar cinnamon syrup in it, then hopped on the counter.

Sebastian nodded his head the way she'd watched one of her uni professors do when about to press an important point. Her husband was getting ready to ask a very deep question. "Tell me one truly rebellious thing you ever did?"

"Hmm." She put her finger on her chin, playfully looking at him. "I need to think about what secrets to give away. Tell me what you did, *Your Highness.*"

Sebastian went to the fridge and pulled out two jars. "Overnight oats made with almond milk and dried fruit."

"Ooh." She grabbed a spoon from the freshly washed rack and opened her container. "So good."

Sebastian took a bite of his, then pointed a spoon at her. "I broke off the relationship with the woman my father wanted me to marry. A year-long affair just..." He snapped his fingers, and a look she worried was wistfulness floated on his features.

A girlfriend. Whoever she was, there'd never been any hint of her in the press.

There was no sign of animosity in his voice. No dismissive tone for a relationship that hadn't worked out. Did he miss her? Was she who he'd really wanted to wear the crown and the reason he'd settled for Breanna?

Words escaped her.

"The night of my first state dinner, I told Samantha that I hated the crown. Hated the responsibility and wished I'd never been born heir to the throne."

He took a deep breath. "And she said she didn't understand that because without it I was a nobody. The crown was the only thing that made me special. Pretty sure it just popped out and she tried to walk it back, but… I could see it was the truth."

That was horrible. "Sebastian." She wasn't sure what else to say. "You—"

"I don't want to talk about Sam. She's gone, and luckily the nondisclosure agreement my father worked out was iron clad. The man had some good ideas."

His voice was set. But the look on his face broke her heart. His title was such a small part of him. But they'd discuss that another time. "Well, that doesn't count."

"Excuse me." Sebastian stepped between her legs, and she dropped a kiss on his lips, happy that he was grinning.

"You broke off a relationship that didn't work. Sorry, Your Highness, but there is nothing rebellious about that. Very standard stuff, actually."

Her husband's eyes rolled to the ceiling. "Fine. I arrived almost three hours late to my first state dinner. It made Briella the villain in a media narrative that still floats to the surface now and then."

Not anymore.

Breanna knew the articles printed about them were less than congratulatory. More than one op-ed had run about the king so openly agree-ing to a marriage of convenience. As though he'd been forced into it, rather than marching into her home after choosing Annie's name from a hat.

Alessio had a lotto bride. King Sebastian had the leftovers. The headlines practically wrote themselves.

"Enough about me. What mischief have you ever gotten up to?"

"I orchestrated my sister's escape."

"Doesn't count." He mimicked her voice, and she couldn't stop the giggle. "I already know that." Sebastian turned the stovetop to Warm, then reached for her hand. "Come one. We can finish breakfast on the patio."

"I told you I changed places with her." Breanna said as she followed him outside. "I didn't tell you that I used a secret fund of money to get her an apartment. That I helped make sure she never has to contact our parents again. Their two-for-one deal is forever outside their reach."

Breanna laughed. "They hadn't fully realized it by the wedding. They refused to talk to her, think-ing that would bring her back. Nope. She's gone. Then my husband—the king—ordered them out." She put her hand to her lips and blew a kiss.

No words fell across the small table for what felt like forever. "I think that counts." She scooped the last bits of oats into her mouth and held up the spoon.

"That isn't rebellion, Breanna." Sebastian's words were soft. "It's survival."

Survival. Three syllables; three tiny daggers she didn't want to acknowledge.

"Want to go into town today?" Breanna pointed to the beach. "It's a beautiful day. Though I suspect every day is beautiful here."

"Breanna—"

"Shopping sounds fun." That wasn't really true. She'd never been a fan of shopping. Except for books and in thrift stores. Those places she could spend hours in.

"We can go shopping later in the week. I have to get security set." Sebastian's brow burrowed as he reached his hand across the table, wrapping it through hers. "But I have an idea."

"More talking…" Breanna had wanted to get to know her husband. Wanted to care for him— it was what she did. But him seeing through her own armor…it was exhausting.

"Yes. But about food." Sebastian put his free hand over his heart. "I am making the curry for dinner, but do you want to make bread?"

"Isn't that baking?" She made a playful face. "I was under the impression my husband did not like baking."

He stuck his tongue out. "I like making bread. But yes, I guess, technically, it's baking. But it's a process. A long one. We can make the dough. Knead it, then sit in the sun or play in the sea while it rises. If you think about it, it's the perfect vacation bake."

"I've never made bread." Breanna ran her thumb along his hand, enjoying the connection but wanting to be away from the chairs, where she seemed intent on spilling secrets she didn't even share with herself.

"But sure."

Breanna beat the dough. Her dough had passed the right stage for rising minutes ago. The bread was going to be hard. But this exercise wasn't about perfect bread. Even hard, it would still be good for croutons and dipping in sauces.

She needed to work out her anger towards her parents. Anger she'd not even allowed herself to acknowledge.

He did, too, but his wasn't decades long. Though if Lucas and Matilda Galanis thought they could profit from having a daughter with a crown, they were sorely mistaken. Money bought lots of things. Power, security, influence.

Things a king had, too. And while he couldn't strip the Galanises of power and security, he could limit their influence significantly. At least in the aristocratic circles they craved. His wife was not part of a "two-for-one deal." She was not interchangeable.

She was amazing, and he was lucky she'd switched places with her sister. His wife sacrificed herself for everyone else. Even a husband she barely knew. From this point forward she needed to be herself. Whoever that was.

"How long am I supposed to beat this?"

"The baking term is to knead." Sebastian chuckled. "Though I think what you have done to that bread counts more as beating than kneading."

Breanna looked up, her mouth falling open. "Wait. Did I do this wrong?"

"Not at all." Sebastian grabbed the oiled bowl he'd prepped for the bread to rise in. "Just put it in here."

Breanna gave him a look he couldn't decipher as she dropped the dough in the bowl. "I feel better." She looked at the dough she'd pummeled, then at him. "Thank you."

"I may not like baking, but making bread is a healing process. Not sure why, but it is true." Sebastian shrugged. He'd created many hard loafs in the last few years.

"You know what else is healing?" Breanna tilted her head, and her fun smile reappeared.

"Should I be worried?" Sebastian saw her hand move to pile of flour she'd used for the bread the instant before it landed on his chest.

"Flour fight!" Breanna giggled as another pile hit his pants.

Flour dust filled the air as he reached for a handful. His toss landed on her shoulder, the dusting cloud dropping specks across her nose and cheeks. She squealed, and happiness burst through his body.

When Breanna grabbed the last handful from the counter, he raised his hands, providing her with a full target. "Give it your best shot, wife."

Wife.

A flash passed over her eyes, but she didn't launch the flour. Instead, she sauntered towards him, the flour tight in her hand. "Husband." She wrapped her arms behind his neck and raised her brows. "There are two options as I see it."

Her husky tone triggered goose pimples on his arms. "And those are?"

"I can drop this flour in your hair. See what you will look like when we have been married for decades and you have passed gray and gone on to white hair."

"That would make quite a mess." Sebastian squeezed her waist. He thought he knew what option two was. And he'd choose it over anything else. But if he was wrong, or she chose to dust his hair with flour, that was fine, too.

"You could kiss me." Pink rushed to her cheeks, but Breanna didn't break her gaze. "Really kiss me."

Sebastian pulled her as close to him as possible. "If I get to choose—" he ran his hand up her back, leaning as close to her as possible "—it is the easiest choice of all." He dipped his head, dropping his lips along her jaw. They were coated in flour, but he didn't want to miss this opportunity.

He took a deep breath, then pressed his lips to hers. This wasn't the hesitant kiss they'd shared right before their wedding. It wasn't the passing glance they'd shared over the altar. Or even the flirty fun they'd had in the sea.

This was the future. It was sweet, passionate, and timeless. Everything he'd dreamed of. Sebastian ran his hand across her skin as his tongue danced with hers as though they'd done this hundreds of times.

She pressed her hands to his back. The handful of flour dropping to the floor behind him... and probably splashing across her skin, too. Another thing that didn't matter.

"Sebastian."

His name on her lips, breathless. Desire exploded through him. He wanted to kiss her, everywhere. Spend the rest of his day worshipping her lips, her body, everything.

She slipped a hand under his shirt. The light touch of her fingers set his skin ablaze. He followed her motion, slipped his hand under her shirt, mimicking each of her strokes.

"We are getting flour all over." Breanna's silky voice matched this moment even though her words were the stuff of comedy.

"We are." Sebastian ached to scoop her up.

One word from her and he'd take her to bed and spend the next several days learning every inch of her. Memorizing what made her sigh with satisfaction and pant with need.

"We could rinse off in the sea." Her lips slipped along his neck.

He'd never had trouble finding words, but when his wife flirted with him, the synapses refused to fire.

"First one to the water wins." Breanna kissed him, then took off running. She was out the door and onto their private beach before he turned.

There was no way he was winning this race, but each of her giggles felt like a trophy.

CHAPTER TWELVE

SEBASTIAN WASN'T BEHIND HER. At least not yet. That final kiss had thrown him, but her husband would follow soon. Still, the delay was the only reason she had the courage to take on the truly rebellious act of dropping her shorts, T-shirt, and bathing suit before racing into the surf.

He'd said she wasn't rebellious. But she could be. She'd show him.

She planned to carve her own path as queen. And she doubted queens took naked dips in the sea after food fights with their husbands.

Turning to the beach, she saw the moment her husband discovered her pile of clothes by the chair she'd occupied most of this vacation. All the momentum he'd had from running evaporated as he looked from the water to her clothes, then back at Breanna. If he'd been a cartoon character, his eyes would have popped out as the sand flew up around him.

She splashed a little but did not rise far enough up for her breasts to exit the water. The bloom of heat she feared was embarrassment was pushing at her mind. Breanna was not going to give in to it. She'd started this. And she was finishing it.

Maybe a rebellious queen was the exactly what King Sebastian needed.

"Come in, the water is very nice. You can keep your clothes on, if you like." He could, but she wanted him to strip. Wanted to run her hands over all of him. Give in to the emotions she felt every time she was near him. Tame the heat that refused to cool whenever his hands were on hers.

The king looked at the pile again, then pulled his shirt off. His abs gleamed in the sun, and Breanna licked her lips.

No one was ever going to say that King Sebastian of Celiana wasn't the most handsome king to sit on the island's ancient throne. His hands went to his shorts. Then he paused and looked at her.

"You will have me at a disadvantage if you leave your shorts on, but I will understand."

I might die of embarrassment, but I'll understand.

Sebastian smiled, then walked into the water. His bathing shorts still firmly on.

Hell.

As he stepped next to her, she fought back the urge to cover herself with her hands. Rebellion wasn't all that good if you didn't commit.

"How is that for rebellion?" She winked, then

slid under the water, running her hands through her hair.

When she surfaced, she raised her hands, patting her soaking hair. "Did I get all the flour out?" Her nipples were just below the surface, but easy to see in the crystal-clear water. And the primary focus of her husband.

He blew out a breath. "Breanna—"

Her name. Only her name left his lips. It was like a meditation as he stared at her.

"Sebastian." She swam a little closer. "You didn't answer my question."

"Question?" He titled his head.

She couldn't stop the giggle. "I *asked* if I got all the flour out of my hair. Aren't you paying attention?"

"I think my wife knows very well exactly what attention she is drawing out of me." The huskiness of his tone sent little waves of desire through her body. She'd never had someone so in thrall to her.

He lifted his head, purposefully looking at her hair. "I don't see any more flour."

"Anywhere?" She twirled, breathing deeply, fearful that her nerve might evaporate any moment.

Sebastian's gargled sound as she spun slowly in the water made her giggle. Power. Excitement. Happiness. In this moment she was simply Breanna. Not one of a pair.

All the emotions swirled in her body as she waited for his answer and met his gaze. "Well?"

His Adam's apple bobbed as he swallowed, then cleared his throat. "No more flour."

She swam close enough that her breasts were nearly touching his chest. "You have a little on your cheek." She dipped her hand in the water, even though it was already wet, then ran her fingers along the streak, wiping it away.

She didn't lower her hand. Instead, she traced her finger along his chin, enjoying the hint of stubble there. "You don't shave as close when you aren't at the palace. I like it."

"Breanna."

There was her name again, followed by nothing else.

"Sebastian." She mimicked his tone. "I like when you kiss me."

His hand was around her waist in an instant. He pulled her close, her body, her naked body, pressed against him. "Your wish, my lady."

She might not have a lot of experience with men—or any—but she understood how the human body worked. Breanna knew how to give herself an orgasm and knew that the bulge on her hip meant her husband was incredibly turned on.

"I think I am going to enjoy having a wife that runs naked into the water. We certainly couldn't do this on a ski slope." Sebastian dipped his head to hers and placed both hands on her butt, lifting her out of the water as his tongue danced with hers.

She wrapped her legs around him. Her body knew what she wanted; her mind would just get in the way.

Waves cradled them as they clung together. Here and now, it was only Breanna and Sebastian. The past, present and future didn't matter.

Nothing mattered except the feel of his lips on hers, the dance of his fingers on her skin.

"Breanna."

Her name sounded different this time. A force rather than a meditation. A breaking. Reality seeping back into their lives.

She pulled back but let her fingers run through his hair. Touching him was a necessity she couldn't understand even as she knew he was about to end whatever was happening here.

"We need to go back inside the cottage." His voice was tight as he pulled back. The moment over.

"Right." She nodded. "The bread is probably ready for the oven."

"I very much doubt the bread is ready for the oven." His lips were so close but not on hers. Not where she wanted them.

Before her brain could muddle through any words, Sebastian continued, "I want you, Breanna. My desire burns. Come to bed with me?"

* * *

"Breanna." Sebastian breathed her name against her ear as she clung to him through the waves. For the rest of time, he'd remember the moment he'd stepped into the sea with his naked bride.

The only reason he hadn't fully stripped was that he'd needed some kind of barrier between him and the stunning sea creature waiting for him in the surf.

"I like how you say my name." Breanna ran her fingers along his chin.

She liked the stubble there, too. His father had instructed him to shave multiple times a day. A prince and king must always be presentable. And stubble or a beard…apparently those didn't fit a royal image.

The first morning, he'd held the razor, then put it away. He was on vacation, after all. In the realm of rebellion, it wasn't anywhere near dancing naked into the sea. But it felt nice.

"Breanna." He let the syllables drip off his tongue before he pressed his lips to the top of her ear. Salt, waves and the scent that was simply his wife invaded his senses. His bedroom seemed so far away, but she deserved her first time to be slow. Sensual. Memorable.

Not a romp on the beach.

"Just like that." Her hands dipped to the waistband of his shorts, her thumb running along the top.

"Again, you have me at a disadvantage. You *are* clothed."

"No." He nipped her ear. "It is *you* who has me at a disadvantage, Breanna." She was the only thing he could think of. Her slick body set his ablaze.

He stepped up to the cottage, and Breanna reached over and turned the door handle.

"Teamwork," she whispered as her fingers ran through his hair.

Teamwork.

He liked that.

Moving through the cottage as quickly as his legs would carry them, Sebastian let her open his bedroom door, and he kicked it closed behind him. Capturing her lips, he gently laid her on his bed.

Stunning didn't begin to describe the siren on his bed. Her wet, dark hair splayed across his pillow; her pink lips were swollen from kisses. Her nipples tightened as he twirled a thumb around each.

"Sebastian."

His name. The power behind the sound of it on Breanna's sweet lips nearly sent him to his knees. Letting his fingers dance across her glorious curves, he listened to each hitch of her breath. Studied each movement that made her arch against him.

Greed was the best description for the urge

within him. But it wasn't his own release he needed. Sebastian craved the knowledge of Breanna's needs. Her wants. The touches that would make her say his name with such perfection.

Dipping his head, he trailed his lips along the same path his fingers had traveled just moments before. Breanna's hips arched, and he took the offering.

His mouth found the right spot, his fingers trailing along the insides of her thighs.

"Sebastian." The pant was perfection as she crested to completion. "Sebastian. I...want... you."

Every bit of control fled his body.

He stood, stripped, and moved on top of his wife. She wrapped her legs around his waist, and it was only as he was pressing against her that the rational thought of contraception broke through passion's fog.

"I don't have a condom." He kissed her neck. This was supposed to be a honeymoon in name only. Only in his dreams had he allowed himself to contemplate this moment.

Breanna let out a breath. "We *are* married, and I have an IUD." She kissed his lips, then pulled back. "But if you want to wait..."

He did not. "Breanna." Sebastian kissed her, joining them and losing himself in the blissfulness that was his wife.

CHAPTER THIRTEEN

BREANNA STRETCHED IN the kitchen. She'd fallen asleep in Sebastian's arms and stayed there until just after six this morning. Her husband was still snoozing. It was the biggest win.

Maybe having company in his bed was what he needed to stay put. If that was a sacrifice she needed to make, it was the best one the universe had ever asked of her.

She smiled as she fixed a cup of coffee for herself and then another for Sebastian. She'd love to let him sleep, but he'd promised her a trip into town. Breanna grabbed a muffin. The top was a little hard. It was still good, but not as fresh as when it had been delivered a few days ago. But neither she nor Sebastian wanted to bake muffins.

It would work for today, and while they were in town, they could make sure they stopped at a local bakery. She'd enjoyed the last several days alone with him. But she was also looking forward to checking out the local bookstore.

Breanna needed to get moving, or rather get

her husband moving. So, she tossed the muffin on a platter she'd found, then headed for the dark room.

"I smell coffee." His words were slow, and his eyes weren't open. The sheet was loosely covering his bottom half.

Her body heated, and the urge to spend the rest of the day right here was nearly overwhelming. But they'd asked security to take them. And a few of the stores in town were planning on their arrival. Inconveniencing others wasn't a good look, especially for royals.

Particularly for such a reason. *Sorry. Can't come, the queen and king are too busy getting busy* wasn't really a statement she wanted anyone to type up.

Sebastian sat up and grabbed the coffee.

He took a deep sip and met her gaze. "I slept in."

"You did." Breanna laughed as he grinned over the mug. "I think we may have found a way to keep your butt in bed."

His eyes sparkled as he looked to her. "I like having your butt in bed." He reached for her, but she pulled back.

"I let you sleep as long as possible, Your Highness!" She tapped the watch he'd given her. "But if I let you touch me…"

She swallowed as he sat up a little straighter. The sheet slipped even further. Her husband, ruffled from a night of good sleep, was sexy as hell.

"If you let me touch you?" His gaze dipped to her breasts.

Her nipples tightened as the memory of him stroking her filled her. "If I let you touch me, you know exactly what will happen."

Sebastian playfully raised his eyebrows twice, then took another sip of his coffee. He was a dream.

"I also brought you a muffin, though it's not super fresh." She held up the platter and tried to remind herself that they had security arriving in less than an hour. That was not enough time to spend in his arms. Though a Sebastian unconcerned about his daily schedule was also hot as hell.

Sebastian leaned forward. His lips met hers, and she melted. Luckily, he pulled back.

"I could get used to my wife bringing me breakfast in bed. Give me one sec." He winked, then slid from the bed, walking to the bathroom.

She didn't look away from his retreating naked form. He was delicious.

Sebastian returned quickly, now wearing a pair of loose slacks, his hair combed but still shirtless. He leaned against the doorframe and looked at the muffin. "I think I'll pass on the three-day-old muffin. We can pick something up in town."

She put the platter on the dresser and wandered to where he was. "Sounds like a plan."

His arms wrapped around her waist, and his

mouth found the spot just below her ear that made her knees go weak. "Sebastian."

"I do enjoy when you say my name." His tongue licked the spot, and then he pulled back. "You're right. We can't start this when today's adventures await us. One of them might even include a bookstore."

"Sebastian." She grabbed his hand, pulling him to the front of the room. A bookstore. Something for her.

"Security is here." Sebastian pointed to his watch. Then the door and the knock followed less than a second later.

"Impressive." Breanna smiled at the security guards as they stepped through the door. It was also sad. Sad that he had his life timed down to the minute.

"Nice to see you." Sebastian nodded to the group as they bowed to him. "My wife wants to spend as much time in the bookstore as possible, and we need to get some goodies from the bakery. But what else is on the agenda?"

Breanna saw the subtle tilt of the security staff's heads. Their dark glasses hid the movement of their eyes, but she wondered if several had raised brows. Sebastian was relaxed. Yes, he was talking about agendas, but not with the stiff air he'd had at the palace.

The head of security nodded to them. "Your honeymoon seems to be going well."

Her cheeks were fire as Sebastian slid his arm around her waist. "My wife has proven to me that vacations are a good idea. We'll have to pencil them in each year." He kissed her forehead.

She knew the head of security was outlining the day. Knew he was explaining the adventures and schedules they needed to keep to. But her brain refused to focus on anything other than Sebastian saying they'd have to pencil in vacations.

He was willing to schedule the vacations. Willing to take time off. Yesterday was fantastic, but today felt like she'd truly won a lottery.

"Ooh." Breanna patted his hand as they walked towards the bookstore. Cameras clicked around them, but his wife's eyes did not leave the blue door of the not-so-tiny bookstore. "This is going to be so fun."

"It is." Sebastian leaned over, kissing the top of her head. Touching her was intoxicating, but watching her get excited for herself brought forth an emotion that there was not a descriptor for.

Stepping through the front door, they left the crowds outside.

"Your Highnesses." The owner of the store and her two employees stepped forward. "We are so glad you came in. I am Lila Patri. Welcome to my store."

Breanna reached for Lila's hands, then the workers standing on each side of her, giving each individual attention as she shook their hands. She was so good at this. Like she was built to be a queen.

"You get to work in one of the best places ever!"

The sincerity of her tone seemed to bring tears to Lila's eyes. "This was my dream as a girl. Owning my own shop full of books from wall to wall. It took until I was fifty to see it to fruition. Spent most of my working life as a public relations manager. Now, though…" The woman gestured to the walls of books; her was happiness clear even if she couldn't put everything into words.

"Dreams are important." Breanna nodded to the owner. "What is your favorite thing about owning the shop?"

Lila looked to him, but he just nodded for her to show his wife around. "I am not sure I can pick just one, Your Highness."

"Breanna. Please, call me Breanna."

He stared at his wife and Lila as they wandered around her store. The king he'd been before they'd gone on this honeymoon would have known down to the minute how long they had to be here. After all, there was a plan for this shopping trip. One he'd asked Raul to work out before their arrival. But Breanna was interested, the owner clearly wanted to show off her store, and he needed a minute to process Breanna's words.

Dreams are important.

Such a simple phrase. One he'd murmured

hundreds of times at events for students, workers, the general public. It was true.

And his wife had never had a dream for herself. Her dreams were all for others.

"Are we ready, Your Highness?" Lila was standing next to Breanna, holding a pad.

"Ready?" His wife looked at him, and the door. "I thought we were browsing for a while."

"You are." Sebastian swallowed the emotions boiling in his throat. Before she could worry there was something jam-packed into their schedule, he grinned. "This bookstore has a fun activity. When I heard about it, I knew you had to try."

Breanna raised a brow. "Activity?"

"Yes." Lila looked like she might bounce away with joy. "This. This is the favorite thing."

"Today." One of her assistants laughed as she gave her boss a big grin. "She says that about all sorts of things."

"Why don't you explain?" Sebastian nodded. She clearly wanted to, and it was her store and activity. No need for him to step in. Though he had a role to play.

"Oh." Lila clapped. "Thank you. I saw a television show once where everyone ran around with a shopping cart. As a kid, I wanted to do it so bad, but in a bookstore."

"You have shopping carts?" Breanna looked at the aisles. They were tiny and stuffed with books.

"No." She bit her lip and leaned in conspiratorially. "I wanted to do it that way, but there isn't room. It was either less aisles or more books."

"Oh, easy choice! Always more books." His wife chuckled, and he thought Breanna and Lila might have been fast friends if she wasn't queen. In this role, there was always a power imbalance that made true friendship nearly impossible.

"Exactly." She motioned to Sebastian. "So, the king is your cart."

He made a show of pumping his muscles, and everyone laughed. "Not sure that is what I was going for." Sebastian made a playful pouty face as Breanna leaned into him.

"You are fine." She kissed him, lingering for just a second. How a few days alone could change so many things.

"You get to walk around for fifteen minutes. Take stock of what you want then. At the end of the fifteen minutes, you get five minutes to pick out as many as you can. The only catch is that Sebastian must be able to carry them all to the checkout without dropping them. Anything in his stack will be twenty percent off."

"Ready?" Sebastian held up his wrist, tapping on the watch. This would be the best use of it he'd ever had. "Set."

Breanna's eyes roamed the store. She was already breathing fast.

"Go!"

She took off. Not running but moving very

quick. She slowed as she reached the romance section and started to pull a few books forward.

"That might be cheating." He laughed as she stuck out her tongue.

"I listened to the rules of this game. No one said anything about not being able to touch the books while I looked around." She raced down the aisle to the general fiction area.

"True." He chuckled as he kept up with her. "Not sure my muscles are going to be able to handle this."

"Better start stretching!" Breanna giggled as she rushed for the hobby section and pulled a few books on sewing and one on crocheting animals. Then it was on to the education section.

There she pulled a few books on early education and lesson planning.

He stopped to look at those titles.

Build Your Classroom for Student Success
Burned Out and Busted: The Road Back for the Exhausted Educator
Everything You Need to Know About Lesson Planning in the Digital World

The titles made zero sense for a queen. She had a degree in education—one she'd never use.

He looked at the three books she'd pulled. Did she want those? She'd wanted to teach. But that was out of her reach now. The queen couldn't walk into an elementary classroom as a regular instructor. It would cause havoc.

Still, there had to be a way to give her something of her own.

"How much time do I have left on my expedition phase?" Breanna was across the store.

He looked at his watch, but before he could answer, Lila called out. "Two minutes twenty seconds, Your Highness."

"Lovely!" She bounced back over to fiction and grabbed a few more titles there. Then raced to the starting line. "Let's go, Sebastian."

"I think you still have a minute or so left?" He looked at his watch as he walked back towards her.

"I know." She pulled one leg up to her back. Then the other. Stretching. "You ready?"

"Honestly?" He shook his head as his wife readied herself. "I'm a little terrified of you right now. Swear you won't hold it against me if I can't carry everything."

Breanna looked him up and down, and playfully held her hands out, measuring his torso. "I think you will do just fine, Sebastian."

"Promise me." This was the first time he'd seen her do something that was just for her. Something she wanted. And if he couldn't carry the whole load. He didn't want to fail at this. Fail her.

She stepped into his arms and kissed him. Lila and the assistants let out a sigh behind them.

"You are going to do fine." She tapped his nose and looked at Lila. "Let's do this!"

Lila could not have asked for a more excited customer. "All right." She nodded to the queen and held up a stopwatch. "You have five minutes, and the king must be able to carry the books."

"Oh, he will carry the books." Breanna laughed and then ran as Lila shouted *Go*.

Books piled into his arms. It was a flash, and he was staggering behind her, letting her shift the books as she added more. Her ability to stack and add was truly impressive even though his arms were burning when Lila called time.

"I can barely see over the top." Sebastian didn't dare laugh or do anything that might jostle the mountain of books in his arms. His muscles were shaking, and he could barely make out the path to the checkout desk, but he was not going disappoint his wife by dropping her precious cargo.

"You just have to set them on the counter." Lila's voice guided his way, but he could hear the surprise in her tone. She was expecting a catastrophe, too.

Breathe. Step. Breathe. Step.

"Almost there." Breanna stood beside him. Calculating the distance or the likelihood of a topple, he didn't know. And there was no way he was turning his head in any way to upset the delicate balance.

Breathe. Step. Breathe. Step.

"Made it." Breanna clapped as he set the pile on the counter. "Nice job." She squeezed him tight, then moved to the other side of her bounty. "Ready for the picture."

"Oh." Lila made another noncommittal noise. "I was under the impression that you didn't want a picture." The proprietor's eyes cut to Sebastian before landing on Breanna.

Breanna pointed to the wall behind the counter. It was covered in pictures of women, men and children posing next to their bounty. None of it quite as hefty as the queen's, but the smiles all brilliant. "It's part of the process, right? I mean…" His wife's gaze cut to him.

"I think Raul thought you might like privacy on your picks." Sebastian shrugged. "You're the queen, after all."

"I want the books shared. I picked local authors, books I have loved, books I look forward to loving, and nonfiction topics that are important to me. These will sell out if people know the queen bought them. Both in Lila's store and online. The authors will reap so much from the free publicity."

"Were any of them your choices?" His tone was rougher than he meant, and he saw Lila step behind the counter, giving them a little distance. This was a gift for Breanna.

For her. Just her.

"Of course." Breanna pointed to the top book.

"This one is a local author that sells at the booths in our market, next to a stall that sells the cutest purses. I think Brie actually has one of the purses. And this topic—" she pointed to the burnout book "—is vital for educators."

She pointed lower. "Did you know there are studies that show most teachers leave the field in the first three years?"

But what about books for her?

"Oh." She grabbed a bright blue one with a winged creature on the front cradling what looked like a human woman. "This one is simply a pure delight of gooey sex that everyone should read. It should be a bestseller in its genre but…" Breanna shrugged.

"So yes, I did pick these for me, but there were other thoughts, too. I am the queen. We have a duty. Something you are so fond of repeating. You chose a queen that wanted the title and the duty that came with it." She huffed and looked around him.

She was right. When he'd walked into her parents' mansion weeks ago, he'd wanted someone who wanted the title. Someone who would let her life belong to the country so she could be called queen. Someone who was doing exactly what Breanna was.

"Sorry, Lila. We don't normally argue in front of people." Breanna bit her lip as color traveled up her neck.

"We don't normally argue." Sebastian added.

"Not sure that is true."

His mouth opened, but he didn't know what to say. Luckily his wife was rushing past it, too.

Breanna pointed to the books. "This was a lovely treat. I got to run around a bookstore picking things out. I got to watch you carry them without tripping, and now, I want to finish this. And yes, it will help others, but these are also my choice."

"But you've already read at least that one." He pointed to the book with the winged creature.

"Yes, but it was downstairs when your people gathered my things. So, I need a new copy. I've reread it at least a dozen times. It's like an old friend. You get it, right, Lila?"

"I do." Lila's answer was quick, and he suspected the shop owner would normally chatter on about all the books she also considered old friends. Dissect what made the characters or plot memorable. Make recommendations for future friends.

None of which she did now. The assistants had disappeared to the stock room. Likely sent there by Lila when this disagreement started. He saw the shop owner look in the back and suspected she was considering if she needed to do the same.

He'd instructed the staff to pick up her room and put her belongings in the suites she occupied in the castle. Told them it needed to be exactly as it had been. A ludicrous order.

And she'd never mentioned that they didn't have all of her things. In fact, the only complaints his wife had issued regarding herself were that her feet hurt. And only after she could no longer stand in her shoes.

Duty was his life, and he'd picked the perfect partner for it. Except he could see the life she'd live. The duty that she wouldn't let overwhelm her like it did him. But that would claw at every part of her life.

Because of him. Because of his title and hers.

"Smile and take the picture, please." Breanna's dark gaze was holding back tears. She'd thought of something lovely. Something helpful. Something that would make a difference in many creatives' lives. And he was trampling on it.

"Of course. I am sorry, Breanna." He stepped next to the books and she stood on the other side.

"Smile." Lila stood in front of them, holding her phone up. "I will post it to social media and then print it for the wall."

She looked at the image, swallowed and then pointed to the stack. "Umm…the light isn't quite right. Queen Breanna can you move your head just a little that way?" She gestured for her to turn her face more towards the books.

It was a trick his father had used frequently. One a public relations manager turned bookshop owner would certainly know. A smile that wasn't as bright could be hidden with the right tilt of the head. The right focus.

He'd stolen his wife's smile with his worries over her books. There was no way for him to kick himself, but he'd find a way to make this up to her. Some way.

CHAPTER FOURTEEN

ROLLING OVER IN her bed, she reached for her husband but knew he was already up. They'd returned to the palace three days ago. And he'd risen well before six each day.

At least he wasn't putting anything on his schedule until eight. It was a small win and one she hoped would stick.

"You're awake." Sebastian swooped in with a breakfast tray and a big smile. At least he still looked rested.

"Yup." She looked at the clock then at him. She wasn't going to ask it directly, but if he volunteered the wake-up time…

"Earlier than yesterday but after five." He shrugged, then set the tray in front of her. "The good thing about me waking early is that I can make you breakfast in bed."

He leaned over, brushing his lips against hers. The quick nature of the kiss left her wanting for more. And as happy as she was to have breakfast in bed…again…she'd prefer to wake next to the man she'd married.

"Today's delight is breakfast tacos. Made with flour tortillas, avocado, seasoned tofu and some cheese." He bowed, so pleased with himself. He was cooking. For her. It was nice.

Sweet.

Before their honeymoon, she'd have given anything to have such attention. Now though. It felt off. Like he was worried she might float away.

She wanted him, but the authentic man.

"Thank you." Breanna looked at the tray. "No plate for you?" There hadn't been one for him yesterday either.

"This is just for you." Sebastian smiled as he moved to open the curtains. Bright rays fell across his face. Light bounced off the hints of blond in his dark hair. Mentally she snapped a picture, wishing her creative side leaned towards painting.

"If you wake at five, wake me. I'll come to the kitchen with you. We can cook together." Breanna took a bite of the taco. It was delicious. Like everything else he made in his personal kitchen.

Sebastian nodded as he looked out the window, but she knew that he wouldn't. He'd sneak out, letting her sleep. Then bring her something sweet or savory.

She finished the taco, grabbed the platter, got

out of bed, and set it on the dressing table. Then she went to where her husband still stood.

"What are you thinking?" She wrapped her hands around his waist, grateful when his fingers locked with hers.

Sebastian took a deep breath. "Honestly?"

"Of course." She wanted the truth, but the breakfast tacos in her belly seemed to flip. "Tell me." She pressed her head to his shoulder, glad that he was turned away from her so he couldn't see the worry she knew was etched on her face.

"I was wondering what you might have done if you'd gotten to teach." He turned in her arms, pulling her close. "If you'd have used your sewing skills to wear fun outfits to go with the lecture."

"Lecture." She laughed. "I was an early education major. I would never have given lectures." She kissed his nose. "Most days I probably would have come home sticky."

He pulled her closer, like he didn't want any distance between them. "I'm serious, Breanna. You would be getting ready right now. Packing a lunch and probably thinking over how to make sure each student excelled for the day. I bet your classroom would have been bright and colorful."

"Annie would have ensured that color was everywhere." Breanna lifted her head, hoping he'd kiss her. Focus on today, on where they were now. Together.

The life he'd described was never going to be

hers. Yes, she'd trained for it. Yes, it was something she'd have enjoyed. Probably excelled at. Yes, her upcycled outfits would have played a role.

In another timeline, in a different place, that Breanna would have been happy.

But this Breanna, the woman she was now in this place, was happy, too.

"I think I'd have enjoyed the classroom. My favorite age was third grade. They are learning to read small chapter books. Still excited to be in school. We'd have painted and sung math songs."

His shoulders slumped.

"But—" she held him tightly "—I am happy here, too." It wasn't hard to say. This wasn't the path she'd have chosen for her life. Maybe that was good.

Life was made from the unexpected. The gifts you didn't know you needed. The people you never expected to fall into your life. To love.

Love.

The word hit her mind, hammering its truth through her. She loved Sebastian. She didn't know how it had happened. How she was so certain that her heart belonged to him.

This wasn't the life she'd asked for. It was better.

"Sebastian." She stepped back and waited for him to turn. "Sebastian."

Finally, he turned, but it was the king standing

here now. The shift was subtle. Less movement in the jaw. Eyes hiding emotions.

"I am happy here. Playing a what-if game can be fun." In the right circumstances, she mentally added. "But it gets us nowhere. After all, what if you weren't the king? Would you be a chef? You'd handle the hours well."

Breanna smiled, but the king didn't show any signs of finding fun in the words.

Instead, he adjusted, like the mantle he'd worn since birth was sliding fully into place. "I never had any choices."

"Neither did I." Breanna lifted her hand, running it along his chin. "But we have choices now."

"Do we?"

"Yes." She didn't stamp her foot, though she desperately ached to add emphasis to the moment. "We are the king and queen."

"I know."

"Do you?" She stroked his chin. The five o'clock shadow he'd worn at the beach house had disappeared the morning they'd packed up to return to the palace. "Do you know that you can choose?"

"Breanna."

She laid a finger over his lips, stopping the argument she saw brewing in his eyes. "You can choose if you wear the title of king. Or if it wears you.

"Here and now, with me, we are just Sebastian

and Breanna. In these rooms, with no one watching. There is no crown. Okay?"

He nodded, and she let out a sigh of relief before removing her finger from his lips.

She replaced it with her lips. He stood still for a minute, then wrapped his arms around her waist.

Breanna drank him in. These moments were the best moments with Sebastian. Her husband. The man she loved. The man she wanted to be happy. They'd wear crowns the rest of their lives. But in this room, with each other, they'd just be Sebastian and Breanna.

"Starting the day with kisses from my wife is certainly my favorite way to begin the day." His fingers caressed her cheek.

He'd started his day alone in the kitchen, but she had no desire to point that out right now. "It's my favorite way to start the day, too."

"Any idea what we are doing for this date night?" Alessio slapped Sebastian on the shoulder as he stepped up to the table Hector had put Sebastian and Breanna's name plate on.

"Nope." Sebastian looked at the tables, each with the name of a couple. Just their name. No titles. "Breanna agreed to this when they were dancing several weeks ago. I guess he bet her that I'd be jealous."

"Were you?" Alessio's gaze went to his wife,

who was laughing with Breanna and Hector over something.

"Yes." There was no need to lie, particularly to Alessio. "I didn't have any reason to be. Not just because there is nothing between Breanna and her friend, but because I didn't really know my wife at the time."

"And now that you know her?" Alessio grinned, his eyes saying there was no need for Sebastian to confirm the feelings.

He looked over to his wife. Annie had joined Hector, Brie and Breanna. The four were in a world all to themselves.

"Quite the group." Beau, Brie's brother, stepped up.

A queen, a princess, the sister of a queen and a party planning entrepreneur. A group bound together by friendship and family. Not titles and rank. Something his wife might have easily had with so many others, if he hadn't marched into her home demanding a bride.

"Any idea what we are doing tonight?" He needed to change the subject. Needed to focus on something, anything other than the feeling that he'd stolen something from Breanna he could never replace.

"Nope." Beau shrugged. "Briella told me to be here. That I was on a 'date' with Breanna's sister, Annie. Whatever Hector has planned is a couple's event, and they needed to round out the numbers. So here I am."

"Brie." Alessio crossed his arms. The nickname was the princess's preferred name and the only one anyone besides her family called her.

Color traveled up Beau's neck as he nodded. "Brie. I know that, and I will get better at it."

Alessio nodded, a man in love with a woman who wanted nothing more than to protect her.

Once more Sebastian's eyes found his bride. She looked over at him, smiled, then waved. The world narrowed to her dark curls, the curve of her lips, the light he knew was dancing in her eyes. All he wanted to do was make sure she had everything.

Was this what Alessio felt when he looked at Brie?

The all-encompassing urge to give her whatever she needed. The desire to make her happy and never let her down.

Love.

He was in love with his wife. With the woman he'd trapped into becoming his queen. A role from which there was no exit.

"You are thinking very deeply." Breanna was beside him, her lips brushing his. "He gets this far-off look when he is worried." She winked at Alessio. "But there are no worries here tonight."

She kissed his cheek and pointed to their table. "Showtime." Her fingers wrapped through his as she pulled him to their table. "This is kind of our first date."

Not kind of. It was their first date. And even in this, she was helping out a friend.

"What are we doing?"

Breanna's face lit up as a group of people, each carrying a box, walked out, depositing the closed boxes on the tables.

"Do not open the boxes until I give the instructions." Hector was standing in the center of the four tables, the ringleader of whatever circus he'd designed.

"You are going to love this." Breanna clapped as Hector gestured to the boxes.

"So, you are in on the activity?" Sebastian put his hand around her waist, enjoying the feel of her laying her head against his shoulder.

"Of course. This is based off some game show he saw a while back. When he told me the plan on the dance floor, I knew we had to be the first to give it a go. There are all sorts of activities, or at least that is his plan, but when he told me about this one—I knew you had to try it." Breanna bumped her hip against his hip. "Now, pay attention."

Hector turned to the table behind him. "Tonight, we cook." He gestured to the three flags on the table. "Sweet. Savory. Spicy. When I say go, one member of your team will run up here and grab a flag. You then have one hour using the items in the box to make a dinner item that is what your flag suggests. Ovens are behind you, and there is a hot plate in the bottom of your box. At the end of the hour, we will judge the dishes, and the winner gets a prize."

Breanna clapped. "This is going to be so much fun. Can I please run?"

"Of course." Sebastian squeezed her tightly. "Try to get anything besides sweet."

"Annie, you and Beau need to get something besides sweet. Otherwise Sebastian will win," Alessio called out. "Unless anyone besides the king is hiding a secret talent for cooking. But the man hates making sweet things."

"Not true." Sebastian stuck his tongue out. "I just don't *like* to make sweet things."

"Not sweet." Breanna stepped beside the table, her knees bent, ready to dash into the fray for him. "Don't worry. I got this."

"Go!"

His wife took off, reaching the table a full second before anyone else. She grabbed the third flag, the savory one, and bounced in front of Alessio, smiling as she headed back to their table.

"May as well pass the trophy to the king and queen now." His brother playfully rolled his eyes as Brie came back holding up the sweet flag with a huge smile for her husband.

Annie had spicy, and she and Beau both looked a little lost as they gazed at the flag and their box.

"Let's do this." Breanna planted the flag and then started pulling things out of the box. "I have no idea what these spices are, but my husband does." She grabbed the chef's hat in the box and placed it on his head. "Tonight, I am your lovely assistant."

His throat closed as the words left her mouth. That was the plan. For her to be his lovely assistant. A queen to get the press off his back. A role anyone could play if they followed the right script. An interchangeable person to give the people of Celiana what they wanted. A lovely assistant.

But she was so much more. So very much more.

"What if you cook tonight?" The words left his mouth before he even knew what he was saying. Lifting the chef's hat, he held it out to her. "You cook, and I will be the lovely assistant."

She looked at the hat, then at him. "You are very handsome, but don't you want to show off your skills?"

"I am here to have a fun date night with my wife. That is all I care about." He kissed her cheek, then set the hat on her head. "That looks good on you. Though everything looks good on you."

She lifted on her toes, pressing a kiss to his ear before whispering, "I think you like it best when I wear nothing at all."

"So true." He leaned toward her, straightening the cap. "Tonight isn't about winning. It's a date night. Just for the two of us."

"I have no idea what I am doing, Sebastian." Breanna held up the rosemary and peppermint. "I mean, I know these are herbs, and this one—" she sniffed the peppermint "—is mint."

"I got you, and you got this." He stepped beside her and looked at the ingredients. "How about a veggie pot pie?"

Breanna looked at the ingredients, too, and then laughed. "I am looking at these like I have any other idea." She gave him a little salute as she giggled. "All right. I'm the cook."

"It almost feels like cheating." Breanna sighed as she sat beside Sebastian on the little couch.

Their pot pie had gone into the oven ten minutes ago. It needed another ten, and then they'd just leave it on warm.

Brie and Alessio were whipping up what looked to be brownie batter with a fancy icing. Annie and Beau hadn't even started whatever they planned to make. Probably not the best sign, but her sister didn't seem overly distressed by whatever was causing their delay.

One of the great things about pot pies was that they only took a few minutes to whip up. Particularly when the host provided a premade pie crust.

"It's hardly cheating." He wrapped his arm

around her. She'd done all the work for the pot pie. He'd supervised the steps, but most of the seasoning she'd done to her taste. And watching her realize that there wasn't an exact recipe—that she could just toss in extra rosemary because it tasted good to her—was one of the top five moments of his life.

And with the exception of Alessio returning home, the other moments all revolved around Breanna, too.

"What if they don't like it?" Breanna looked over at the oven, the minutes counting down.

"They will." He squeezed her shoulder and kissed her head. "They will like it."

"And if they don't, they probably won't tell me." Breanna laughed.

"Probably not." Sebastian let out a sigh. "One hardly ever tells the king and queen the truth."

His wife sat up, her eyes wide and hurt. "Sebastian, I meant that our family and friends would spare my feelings. They would ooh and ahh over the dish, as I will for theirs. Not because of their titles."

"Right." Her words made sense, of course. Even if he wasn't sure they were the complete truth. Alessio rarely spared his feelings, but in a group...in a group he'd defer until later. Beau, Annie and Hector. He doubted they'd see more than the crowns that were metaphorically always attached to Breanna and his heads when critique time came around.

"No." Breanna sat up straighter. "No, this isn't a 'right,' moment."

"I like it when you use air quotes." He winked, looking over her shoulder to see if anyone was noticing the disagreement going on. Alessio and Brie now had piping bags out. Annie and Beau were studiously cutting up something at their table with Hector by their side, laughing and trying to break the clear tension between the two of them.

Breanna looked over her shoulder, too, then back at him. "Worried someone might hear us arguing? It's one of the things we do best." She crossed her arms and shook her head. "These are our friends and family. Here, you are Sebastian, not the king."

"I'm always the king, Breanna." He let out a heavy sigh, hating how he'd soured the evening. "As you are always the queen. And arguing isn't what we do best."

Why did she keep bring up their tendency to spat?

"I said one of the things." Breanna patted his knees. "It's not a bad thing."

"Arguing is bad." It was the definition of the word. His parents had never argued. In fact, he didn't remember seeing any kind of disagreement. They'd lived separate lives, but when they were together, it was not quite peaceful but serene enough.

"No." The timer dinged on the pot pie, but Breanna didn't move. "Arguing is communicating. And when done in a healthy fashion, it's positive. We don't yell at each other. We don't scream. We discuss. We hash things out. That is healthy."

"Somehow I can't imagine the Galanis patriarch and matriarch having solid communication capabilities." The few times he'd seen her parents together, the loathing they had for the other was hardly kept at bay. In fact, he was fairly certain the only thing keeping them together was the mutual desire for more wealth, and probably spite.

"They didn't." Breanna blew out a breath. "I took a family communications class in university. Parents can get miffed when teachers give feedback that their children are less than perfect."

The timer continued sounding. "We need to get the pot pie out."

"We do. But this is more important. You are more than your crown, Sebastian. I don't know why you can't see that. And your wife pointing it out, not fighting but arguing with that belief, is healthy dialogue."

He could see Alessio looking at the oven with the time. Then his brother glanced over at the couch, his eyes widening before turning back to the brownies. "Breanna, we can discuss this at the palace."

"This is family and friends. We aren't fighting. We aren't yelling. We are talking. They aren't listening any more than you are listening to whatever argument Annie and Beau are having right now."

Annie and Beau were working on their own. Neither appeared to be saying anything, and her back was towards them. "They aren't arguing."

"Yes. They are. I can read Annie like Alessio can read you." Breanna stood up. "The people that matter see you. Just you. But if you can't see past your crown, then that is one you." She moved towards the oven.

"Oh. It bubbled over. It will probably still taste good, but it looks a fright."

"So do the brownies!" Brie called, her laugher echoing in the room.

"My cheese dip will *actually* be spicy, but it looks a little like yellow mud," Annie responded, her eyes cutting to Beau.

Alessio held up a brownie that could only be described as a mess. "I don't know. I think this is gorgeous. It could fetch a nice price at the farmer's market."

"Only because you are the heir to the throne." Brie kissed her husband.

It was funny…because it was true.

And forgetting it wasn't an option.

CHAPTER FIFTEEN

"You sure you're okay with Alessio and me going up to the ski slopes today?" Sebastian looked at his calendar.

He wasn't surprised that Breanna had wedged a day off into it, but he was a little shocked at how much he wanted to go.

"Why wouldn't I be?" She kissed his nose as she looked at her calendar. "I have more than enough meetings to keep me busy." She stuck out her tongue and laughed. "Go. You deserve a day on the slopes. And you will have more fun with Alessio than you will with me."

A knock echoed on the chamber door. "That will be your brother."

Alessio stepped in a moment later. "Hey, um, Brie is a little under the weather. We think it's because…" Alessio pulled at the back of his neck, color traveling up his neck.

"Because?" Breanna clapped; she'd seen Brie make a face after smelling Annie's cheese dip the other night. She probably should have warned people that Annie could put fire on her tongue and think it needed a bit more kick. She didn't want to assume, but she thought she knew what Alessio was getting ready to tell them.

"What?" Sebastian looked from Breanna to his brother. "I feel like I am missing something."

"Brie's pregnant."

"Yes!" Breanna danced over to Alessio, gave him a hug, and then stepped back to let Sebastian have the time with his brother.

"Congratulations. Did you want to stay off the slopes today?"

"No, but since we aren't certain that the illness is pregnancy-related, she wanted me to give you a choice about coming. I think she wants me out of the house. I am a worrier, according to my wife."

"That makes sense. I still want to hit the slopes, if you do. And now we can talk baby things." Sebastian slapped his brother on the back, then came over to her.

He kissed her deeply, "Thank you for setting this up. I—"

For a second, she thought he might say the words she craved hearing. But instead, he pushed a curl behind her ear and kissed her cheek.

"I will see you when I get back."

"I don't think the flu that captured Brie and Alessio is going to spare me." Sebastian let out a sigh as he lay in bed. His wife was snuggled next to him.

"You are burning up." She pressed her lips to his cheek.

"I don't feel hot." It was kind of true. The chills wracking his body refused to take any of the heat pouring over his head. He felt cold…and then hot…and then freezing.

"I think you should accept that you need a sick day." She kissed his forehead, then pulled back. Breanna climbed out of bed and grabbed her phone. She typed something out quickly. "Any chance there is a thermometer in your bathroom?"

Fog coated his brain, trapping words. Plucking them out of the mental ether was exhausting. "Why would I have a thermometer?"

Breanna clucked her tongue and muttered something under her breath.

"All right. I've canceled your engagements for the next two days. Do not argue with me."

Even if he wanted to, there was no charge in his battery. Maybe he could still manage some correspondence from bed.

A knock sounded at the door, and Breanna stepped to it. "Raul, is that you?"

"Yes, Your Highness."

"Did you bring the thermometer?" She still hadn't opened the door.

"Yes. And the other things you requested."

He wanted to ask what else she'd requested, but his eyes were so heavy. A short nap and then he'd text Raul to bring any papers he needed.

"Thank you. Please leave them at the door and back away. I've already been exposed, but no sense having the staff take more risk than necessary." She waited a moment, then opened the door.

He heard her say something about schedules and thought he heard his mother's voice. But then the nap won.

Breanna kissed her husband's forehead, thankful that he was cool. Day three of their lock-in and he was finally turning a corner. Sebastian's fever had broken last night. But he was still exhausted.

He was rounding the cusp, as she tried to ignore the tickle in the back of her throat and the sweat at her temple that she knew meant the virus was on her heels now.

Smoothing the dress she'd asked Raul to bring her, she stepped into the king's suite. Which now had her sewing machine and her latest project to help her pass the time.

She checked herself in the small mirror and smiled. It was a silly alphabet dress that she'd made when she was student teaching. The ABCs were splayed in no real pattern. A few pencils and apples were sprinkled in for good measure.

One did not put it on unless you were a teacher. The kids she'd taught as a student teacher had loved this dress. And the others she'd made. It was cliché, but she enjoyed dressing up for her class. At least as queen she could reuse the outfits when she did outings for small children.

She'd been scheduled to attend a primary school today. The students were putting on a poetry reading they'd worked for weeks on. Seven- and eight-year-olds took their writing as seriously as any national poet. She was to be the exalted guest. The kids were excited to read to a queen.

But there was no way she was risking little bodies with what the doctor had confirmed was influenza. Particularly since she was fighting her own battle with it now.

Still, she'd asked Raul to check with the teacher to see if there was a way for her to attend virtually. The woman was apparently very open to it, but as soon as the virtual call was over, Breanna was crawling into bed.

"Good morning, class." The teacher's voice echoed over the computer.

She'd been instructed to keep her computer screen off until she was announced since the kids thought she'd had to cancel. A good plan in case she'd been too busy taking care of Sebastian. Or too sick herself.

"Today we are reading our poems, and I have a special surprise." The teacher clapped, and the squeals her students let out on the word *silence* stopped. A well-run classroom.

"Remember how the queen was supposed to come?"

A chorus of yeses echoed through the speaker. Little voices that brought an immediate smile to Breanna's face. She'd have enjoyed the life of teaching.

"Well, she is taking care of the king, who has the flu, but…" The teacher did a little drumroll on her desk, and the students followed.

At the top of the roll, Breanna started her camera and then waved to the room full of excited kids. A cough built in her throat, but she smiled through it.

Was this what Sebastian always did? Probably.

"So, we are going to read our poems for the queen after all." The teacher looked at the camera, bowed her head. "Who wants to go first?"

Most of the room's hands shot up. The teacher laughed, walked to her desk, and picked up what looked to be a decorated tin can with popsicle sticks. "You know the rules. If I call your name, you can pass, but you don't get another chance to go until everyone else has gone."

She drew the first name, and a little girl with pigtails and a blue dress stood up. She read a devotion to her cat—Pickles.

After that was a funny poem about a little brother that the boy didn't want but was learning to love. And then another poem about a pet, a rabbit this time.

The afternoon wore on. It was fun and great, but the throbbing in her head, the pain in her throat, the aches in her bones grew with each passing second. But her smile never dropped.

When the final child rose to give her reading, Breanna was taking strategic breaths through her nose to keep the coughing fit at bay.

A few more minutes. A few more minutes. Hang on. Do not interrupt this child's experience. She gets the same as her classmates. A few more minutes.

The mantra repeated in her mind as she kept the smile on her face. When it was finally over, she waved one last time, knowing that if she said anything, it would be covered by coughs.

Shutting off the camera, she let out a shudder, and then the coughs erupted. Her body rocked as she tried to gain any semblance of control, but the coughs refused to abate.

"Honey." Sebastian's arms wrapped around her shoulders, gently lifting her up.

All of a sudden, there was no way to ignore the ache in her bones. She let out a little cry, but Breanna was pretty sure the coughs covered it.

"Into bed. I'll get you some lemon tea, but rest is what you need." Sebastian guided her to his room.

"Do you want me to go back to my room?" The words were garbled. The brain fog her husband had talked about seemed to leap from his brain to hers. She honestly wasn't certain she'd make it down the hall.

"You are in your room. Our room." He kissed the top of her cheek as her head traced the pillow. "You really pushed yourself for those kids."

"I needed to." They'd worked so hard. They'd been promised a royal, and... Words evaporated, and she wasn't even sure she'd gotten them all out.

"Uh-huh. I get it." His voice was far away. Dreamlike words. "And now you do, too."

Sebastian's lips were cool on her burning forehead. There were words she needed to say. A thought she wanted to get out. But no matter how hard she tried to grasp at it, the darkness pushed it farther away.

CHAPTER SIXTEEN

SHE WASN'T SURE how long she'd lain in this bed, but Breanna did know that she had no desire to spend another moment in it. Pulling off the coverings, she gave herself a shake. There were three things she wanted to do. Find her husband. Take a shower. And put on new clothes.

Preferably in that order, but at this moment, she didn't particularly care.

Stepping into the study, she wasn't surprised to find Sebastian at the desk she'd pushed out of the way for her sewing machine and fabrics back in its rightful spot. The mountain of paperwork was disheartening but not unexpected, either. "Did you take any time for yourself while I've been under the weather?"

Sebastian's head popped up. His hand moved too quickly, and the bottle of ink he was using to sign documents tipped.

"And that is why you need to put the lid back on if you insist on using a fountain pen dipped in ink." Breanna didn't laugh—her chuckle was too likely to bring on a cough—but she smiled so her husband knew she meant it as a joke.

Sebastian was at her side, ignoring the spill and the other documents it would wreck.

"Your desk will get stained." Breanna looked over his shoulder, but he just raised his hand to her forehead and let out a sigh.

"No fever." Laying his head against hers, he pulled her close. "And the desk has a hundred years' worth of stains on it." He kissed her head. "Want a shower?"

"Do I stink that bad?" She laughed, and a small cough followed, but at least it no longer wracked her body.

"You are gorgeous, even minutes past your sickbed, but the first thing I wanted when I got up was to see you and then to shower."

To see you.

She'd felt the exact same thing.

I love you.

The words were on the tip of her tongue, waiting to drop. Still, she held back.

Why?

Maybe because she didn't want to say it while she still looked a fright from her own flu battle. Maybe...

Sebastian gazed at her, like he, too, had words that wouldn't fall.

Shower—then—then it was time to tell her husband how she felt.

* * *

Sebastian stood in what until yesterday was his reading room and desperately tried to control the anxious wobbles in his soul. This had seemed like such a good idea after the headlines regarding Breanna's "choice of outfit" for the poetry reading. The fashion columns had critiqued the ABC dress no end. The reviews online were mostly positive. But the main headlines discussed the reviews that weren't. Plastered them up front before pointing out that even the fashion icons who claimed to hate the dress admitted that it was a good option for a children's poetry event.

The cut. The tailoring. Everything she'd worked on had been pulled apart.

Because he'd fallen ill, she was sitting in the palace rather than in the classroom. Maybe if she'd attended in person, she'd have been spared most of the comments regarding her attire.

But that wasn't the only thing they'd discussed. A few podcast interviews had dissected her look on the camera. How she'd seemed focused elsewhere. Things that should have stopped the moment the palace announced she was under the weather.

Instead, the news had buzzed that the palace was crafting that narrative to give her peace after she'd looked "bored" with the children.

The thing she loved most, along with her love

for children, tarnished because he'd taken a day off at the ski slopes.

He'd had to do something.

The buzz around the dress, and the fact that no one knew his wife's talent, spurred this room. She could use it to create and maybe...just maybe to teach, too. At least online. A little piece of the dream she'd once wanted, even if she hadn't put it into words for herself.

He'd put out a statement regarding the dress and the fact that the queen had made it. That most of her garments, even her wedding dress, were crafted on machines with love by her own hands.

That had sent the news cycle into a spiral. And stopped the news about her appearance at the school. Glowing articles about a queen making her own wardrobe. Creating her own custom pieces. The negative statements had eased away. And now one of the articles praising her was framed and hanging on the wall, next to a ring light and recording equipment.

She was too talented to hide this. Too special to let this gift go unnoticed. This could have been her dream. If she'd just allowed herself to have one.

He couldn't undo the crown on her head. But he could give her a dream that was for her. Show her this and then tell her how much he loved her. How lucky he was that she was his queen.

"What?" Breanna's voice hit his back. "Your reading room—"

"Never got used anyway. So..." He spun, showing off the racks of fabric the staff had carefully shifted from her old rooms. "And don't worry, they all came through the outside door. No one else got the flu."

That was an impressive feat. One he never would have thought of. But his wife had jumped into action, keeping everyone away to protect them and care for him. The woman never thought of herself. So, this was for her. Something that was Breanna's.

She looked at the machines, each in a separate area. One of the staff was into fabric works and was able to help the team understand why aesthetics weren't as important as function, with each machine having a designated place and role to play.

"Wow." Breanna's hand covered her mouth. "This. This is..." Whatever she planned to say dropped away as her eyes found the framed article and ring light.

Time slowed as she stepped towards it, shaking her head.

"Breanna—"

"Why is there an article about my sewing? You framed it?"

Tears coated her eyes, but he couldn't understand why. Her skill. Her creativity. Those were worthy of praise. So much more than just the crown on her head. "People were writing articles about the queen looking upset at the poetry event. Bored. And there was a lot of focus on the ABC dress. The headlines before I told them about this were rather unflattering."

"Unflattering to the crown." Her words were soft, broken.

This was not how this was supposed to go. "I'm proud of the work my queen does. I want the world to know that the queen is talented." This was Breanna.

"My queen." Breanna let out a breath. "That is all I am, isn't it?"

"We had to answer, Breanna. Make them understand the queen—"

"No, we didn't." Breanna bit her lip, shaking her head. "And *we* didn't answer. You answered. Without talking to me."

Okay. That was a fair assessment. And one he'd worried over—apparently with good cause. "You were ill. The headlines…"

"Right. The headlines. The king and queen must respond. It is our duty to be available. Always available. Everything we do belongs to the country."

"I was proud of you. Your work is so impressive, and you were ill but smiled through it." Wrong words.

"What I meant was—"

"I know what you meant. I finally stepped fully into the role, right? The all-encompassing crown, serving even when I was far too ill." His wife crossed her arms and looked down at the ring light. "Lighting for me to show off on what, the palace social media? Or do I have to run my own video streams now, so that everyone can see what *the queen* can do?"

How had this gone downhill so fast? This was a gift. A surprise.

"No. You don't have to *do* anything. But the country—"

"The country comes first. Everything is for Celiana. Even the one thing I told you was for me. Mine. The thing I didn't share."

Sebastian pointed to the article. "Do you know what they were running before this piece? They were breaking down the cut. Discussing the neckline and why you would choose such a silly design."

"Who cares?" Breanna damp curls bounced as her bottom lip quivered. "I asked—no—I told you that this was mine. Weeks ago. Before I..." She bit her lip so hard, he worried blood was coating her tongue.

"We have an image. A duty. This humanizes you. It gives..."

"I don't care. In these rooms, I told you I just wanted to be Sebastian and Breanna. Just us."

Brenna wiped a tear from her eye. "This is my job. It is not who I am."

It wasn't that simple. It would be nice if it was. But they were the king and queen everywhere. Even when they didn't want to be. Everything was tinted with the golden hue of their crowns. "You are the queen. You married the king. This is your life. We are the king and queen. It is all we are."

She'd done so well the other day. Hiding her illness to make the students happy. It was what a queen did. What a royal did. She'd truly become the queen that day.

Breanna turned, looking at the image on the wall. The article he'd been so proud of now destroying the gift he'd wanted to give.

"You're right. This is my life. I am the queen." She sucked in a breath.

Words he'd ached for her to say. Words he wanted her to believe, but her tone, the resignation in it, destroyed him.

"It's a role anyone could play, if they knew the script."

"Breanna—"

"I am going back to my rooms, Your Highness." There was no emotion in her tone. No fire. No spirit.

"Because you want to?"

"What I want doesn't matter. It's all for the crown. You showed that." Breanna pressed her hand to his shoulder as she started past him. "For what it is worth, until just now, you were never just the king, in my eyes."

Her words nearly broke him. But he needed her to understand. "I still am more than the king for you. But wanting more, a life outside the crown, that only leads to heartache, Breanna. We are royal. We are—"

"The king and queen of Celiana. I know." Her words were soft, and then she was gone.

CHAPTER SEVENTEEN

"THANK YOU FOR complimenting my dress. I didn't make it. It is the work of a young man named Mathias who is apprenticing at Ophelia's. Yes, he does amazing work. One day everyone will know his name." The queen's voice carried next to him as she shook hands with another guest who was hoping she'd made the stunning purple floor-length gown.

His eyes had bounced out of his head the moment she'd stepped into the room tonight. The first time he'd seen her all day. A common occurrence over the last week. Breanna was never late to her appointments.

As queen, she sparkled. Shining far brighter than he ever did. But the sparkle was fake. The smile plastered in place. Others might not be able to tell, or maybe they could and didn't care.

Her sewing equipment, or was it tools…crafting lingo was foreign to him…whatever they were, were still in his suite. She hadn't touched them all week.

Breanna had become the ghost he'd promised she could be when she took the crown. Separate lives. And he was dying inside.

"If you'll excuse me, my dear. I need to get a drink. Do you want to come?" A soft shake of her head was all she gave him.

Barely an acknowledgment. It stung. A week ago, he'd have leaned in and kissed her. Flitted her away for a break. Now...a wall of his construction stood between them. "I shall bring one back for you, too."

Breanna nodded, but she never turned her attention away from the guest in front of her.

"She plays the role well." His mother slipped her hand through his arm, walking in step as they headed to the refreshment stand.

Role. The thing he'd wanted Breanna for. What a fool he'd been walking into that compound. A name from a hat. The wrong name. "She shouldn't have to play a role."

"All humans play roles." His mother's voice was soft as she took the glass from the waiter and then lifted it to her lips before looking around. "The question is, do we play the role we want or the one expected of us."

Sebastian didn't bother to hide his chuckle. "We." He downed the drink. "*We* don't get a choice."

His mother tilted her head, her eyes landing on the other side of the room. Alessio and Brie were chatting with someone. Her hand was protectively over the bundle of joy they'd shared with the palace but not the world yet. And the flu that had crippled them had done no harm to the precious little prince or princess arriving in seven or so months.

"They chose." His mother squeezed his hand. "The plan for them was to have a marriage of convenience. A fake love story, just like your father and me. But they chose a different path. A better path." Sadness passed over her eyes but no tears.

"Did you want more with father?" King Cedric only cared about Celiana. It was his greatest trait. And largest failing.

The dowager queen looked at the couples on the dance floor and sighed. "I didn't know there was more to want. But there is, Sebastian. You will always be the king to the country. To the world."

"But." He wanted there to be a but so badly. Needed a but.

His mother's eyebrows lifted. "But?"

Sebastian's ears rang, and heat cascaded over his face. "But in the palace, with the people I love, I get to choose."

Such a simple statement. One his wife had told him over and over again. And then he'd stolen the thing she was keeping for herself. Given it to the country, while she was sick and unable to voice her wants.

Her wants.

Her family had refused to let her have her chosen career field. Her chosen spouse. And she'd stayed happy. Chosen happiness for her sister. Chosen happiness with the husband who'd pulled a name out of a hat.

Been something different in a world that just wanted to see her as a cookie-cutter image. She'd been different, too. Until he'd turned her into what she was now.

"I messed up. God, that doesn't even cover it. I screwed up." Castigating himself might feel good. But it didn't do any good.

He was going to make this up to her. And tell her what he should have told her a week ago. He loved her. Loved Breanna, not the queen. Just her.

"I am stealing my sister." Annie grabbed Breanna's hand as she led her from the never-ending receiving line. "Go dance!" her sister yelled to the gathered and flabbergasted crowd.

Breanna was glad for the reprieve and shocked by the deliverer. "Annie."

"Don't look so surprised. You needed saving."

"And no one else was going to do it." Breanna bit her lip as the bitter words welled up. She'd played the queen all week. The perfect attendant. The person her husband had married her to be.

She'd spent her life looking for the bright side. Grasping at every silver lining. A week of this was killing her. What would a lifetime look like?

"Sebastian offered you a break."

Breanna shrugged. That was true. Maybe. But being in his presence hurt too much. The man was the king first. He'd made that clear. And she was the queen. Trapped in a life of her own making. She'd make the same choice again, for Annie.

But she'd guard her heart. Some way.

"The king is back in the receiving line."

Back right after I left.

That didn't hurt. It didn't.

Maybe one day it wouldn't, but right now... "That is his job. His purpose."

"And what is yours?" Annie squeezed her hand.

"What?" Her giggle was nerves, but the question landed in her heart. "What?"

"You already said that." Annie led them through the garden. "Repeating it doesn't change my question. What do *you* want? And you can't say anything about my safety or security. You can't say something about your husband. Or a friend. What do you, Breanna, want?"

"I don't understand the question."

"Yes, you do. You're scared of the answer maybe, but you know what you want. Just like I know that Mathias helped with that dress, but it is your design. Your fabric—its reclaimed from a piece you found after the high school dance season. If the young woman who'd worn the original design knew it was on the queen, she'd squeal with delight."

Breanna ran her hand over the fabric. The original gown was a ball gown with so much tulle Mathias and Ophelia had used it to create two wedding veils. "This is mine. Something that is just mine. No one can take—"

The words were out, and Annie hugged her as a sob wracked her body.

"Sebastian wasn't taking it." Breanna squeezed her eyes shut, the truth shaking her. He was trying to give her something. Something she would not have reached for for herself.

"No. He was bragging on you. A weird feeling when no one has ever done it." Annie pushed a tear away from Breanna's cheek. "It's a good thing you have waterproof mascara."

"He should have talked to me." Breanna was grasping. She knew that. She'd have told him no. Told him that he couldn't. Even if part of her wanted the world to know. To display the benefits of sustainability in a world focused on consumerism.

"Yes, but would you have listened?" Annie was always good at knowing her sister's internal thoughts.

So much so that Breanna didn't even pretend to give an answer other than sticking her tongue out.

"That is what I thought." Annie hooked her arm through Breanna's. "Another thought, if you'll allow it."

"Do I have a choice? You didn't used to be so pushy." Breanna squeezed her sister. This was a good thing.

"My sister gave me wings," Annie beamed as she guided them back to the ball room. "But that isn't my thought. It's this: If you didn't love him, would it have hurt? You don't have to answer to anyone but yourself. But our parents can snipe at each other, then push through their next big project as a team because they don't care about each other. They care about themselves and found a partner willing to go along."

"I never said I loved him." Breanna had kept that realization to herself. Even if part of her wanted to shout it to the entire world.

"It is clear to anyone who looks. You love him. He loves you. You've hurt each other. You have two choices now. Live in this role bitter and alone. The country will be fine and most probably won't notice that you two ache being near each other. You will know. Always."

Breanna shuddered. "Or we carve our own paths together."

Annie smiled and pushed her into the room. The receiving line was longer now than it had been when she left. How was that possible? How did so many people want to spend so much time in line rather than enjoying themselves at a party?

Sebastian caught her gaze before she got to her place. She saw more than a few heads turn as he walked past the line he always stood in until the last person arrived. When he'd asked if she'd wanted a drink, she'd purposefully said no to try to get through this faster.

"Breanna." Her name was soft on his lips.

The room was watching, but all she could see was the man before her. The dark circles under his eyes. Her hand went to his cheek. "You don't look like you're sleeping."

"I'm not." He placed his hand over hers. "Dance with me?"

"The line…"

"Dance with me, please?" Sebastian asked again.

"All right." She placed her hand in his.

He squeezed it tightly. "The queen and I are dancing. The receiving line is over. Come join us on the floor. Let's have a good time."

"Over?" Breanna couldn't help the laugh. "Really, Your Highness. I thought that was our duty."

"Breanna, we have roles to play, but I never want to be anyone but Sebastian to you. As for duty, we have been in that line for almost two hours. I want to dance with my wife. Hold her. Tell her how sorry I am. This isn't the right place. I know that. But I can't wait. I don't want to."

Her mouth was open. There were words she should say. But her mind was firing too fast to find any.

"I should have waited to ask about the sewing. I am just so damn proud of you. And I wanted to show you off for something that had nothing to do with the crown. And yet I made it about the crown. I—"

She laid a finger on his lips. "I know. It took me time to see it, and one very pushy twin sister. But I know. I've hidden all my life. Worried that others just see me as an interchangeable twin. But I don't want to hide anymore. I'm the queen, but so much more."

"And I am the king and so much more."

Her lungs exploded as she cried, "Yes." Several heads turned towards them. Alessio and Brie were watching and grinning.

"In these walls and together, we play the role we want. And I want to play the role of a man who loves his wife. Crown or no crown." Sebastian ran one hand over her cheek as he pulled her closer with the other.

"I love you, too. Just you. Just Sebastian. You could throw away the crown, the palace, everything, and I would still love you."

His head lay against hers. "I love you. I love you. I will never tire of saying that."

"I certainly hope not." Breanna let him spin her around the room. "I love you, too."

EPILOGUE

"As you can see, needing to rip out a stitch happens to everyone. Even those of us who have created more garments than they can count." Breanna laughed as she held up the seam ripper to the video conference she was running from the sewing room next to their suite.

She hosted one of these monthly and had worked with Ophelia and Matthias to train a few teachers on the art of upcycling. And then worked with thrift stores to ensure that they didn't drive up the cost of their clothes just because more people were thrifting now.

It was amazing to watch her emerge from the protective shell she'd kept herself in.

"Oh, Sebastian is here, do you want to say hello?" Breanna stepped aside as he moved to where the group could see him.

A few members of the class raised their heads to wave, but most kept the focus on their projects. The aura of the throne had diminished in the last year as the people came to see the king and queen more as people than fairy-tale creatures.

Now there was a deeper connection with the populace and a palace that finally felt like a home. All because of the woman beside him— who the class really wanted to see.

"All right. Work your projects, reach out to the mentors if you have questions, and I will see everyone next month." Breanna waved and then clicked off. "One woman found that she doesn't like sewing nearly as much as knitting. So she is taking apart knitted sweaters and reusing the yarn. I didn't even know that was possible. It's really cool; she was talking about it at class when she explained this would be her last one. I need to reach out to Raul and see if he can get her contact information. I bet there are other yarn workers who would be interested in learning her technique."

"I bet there would be." Breanna's drive and care for others was invigorating, "But I didn't barge into my wife's studio on our day off to talk about projects. Well, not true, I came to talk one project in particular."

"You never barge in. You are always welcome." Breanna kissed his cheek. "What project?"

"Our anniversary is coming up, one year." The best year of his life.

She glanced at him as he looked over the fabric. "Our wedding day wasn't the best." He kept his tone upbeat, but he'd always regret that she hadn't gotten the day she deserved.

"Wasn't the worst. We had a good time."

His wife, ready with the silver lining. "I thought maybe you'd like a do-over. A vow renewal, just with our family and friends. To say all the things I wish I could have said at the altar the first time. With a dress and suit made by you?"

"I already have a dress. I think wearing the same one would be a nice touch. But as for a suit…" She bounced as she grabbed her tape measure. "I have the perfect idea. Ooh!" She danced around him, wrapping his body with the tape measure, taking notes.

Sebastian grabbed for her wrists as the tape measure slid up his thigh and her fingers wandered with it. "Still taking measurements?"

Breanna's eyes lit up as she dropped the tape. "I think this would be easier with your pants off."

"My queen." He bent, capturing her lips, then lifting her off her feet. "We have all afternoon free, and I plan to spend it with you."

"In bed?"

"Your wish is my command."

* * * * *